Treasures of the Taylorian:
Series Two: Writers in Residence
Volume 4

Hedwig Dohm

The Woman You Become

Werde, die du bist!

Translated by Emily Dicker,
Victoria Mckinley-Smith,
Lia Neill, and Isabella Reese

Edited by Marie Martine

Series Editor: Henrike Lähnemann
Taylor Institution Library, Oxford, 2025

Taylor Institution Library
St Giles, Oxford, OX1 3NA

http://editions.mml.ox.ac.uk

© The Translators

Digital downloads for this edition are available via https://editions.mml.ox.ac.uk/publications/.
They include a pdf eBook of the text.

Typesetting by Henrike Lähnemann
Cover design by Emma Huber
Cover image and artwork by Emily Dicker

ISBN 978-1-0686058-3-3

Printed in the United Kingdom and United States
by Lightning Source for Taylor Institution Library

Table of Contents

Previous volumes in 'Treasures of the Taylorian'
Open access available at https://editions.mml.ox.ac.uk/publications/

Preface

As editor of 'Taylor Editions', it is a pleasure and honour to introduce this collaborative translation of Hedwig Dohm's novella as the newest contribution to series 3 'Writers in Residence'. 'Werde, die du bist!' is translated by four second-year students and edited by my colleague Marie Martine at The Queen's College. The four *Studentinnen* reflect on their feminist approach to the task in their 'Translators' Introduction'.

This form of reflecting on the consequences of translation choices for literature is a core part of the Oxford curriculum, and it is also the ideal continuation of a series which started in 2016 when Ulrike Draesner offered her 'radical translation' of seventeen Shakespeare sonnets with their 'radical back-translation' into English as a contribution to the exhibition 'Shakespeare in Translation' in the Taylorian Library.

The second volume of the series continued the theme of women and translation, as it brought together students of German, Japanese, English, and History of the Book for a translation workshop with the Japanese-German author Yoko Tawada and an exhibition 'Von der Muttersprache zur Sprachmutter' on multilingual writing.

More recently, a final year student of German, Tara Williams, contributed an anthology of text and images conceived during her Year Abroad in Bamberg as an homage to E.T.A. Hoffmann. It seems logical to take this student-led approach even further and have second-year students publish their own translation for the first time.

May it be the start of many more volumes in the series!

Henrike Lähnemann
Oxford, June 2025

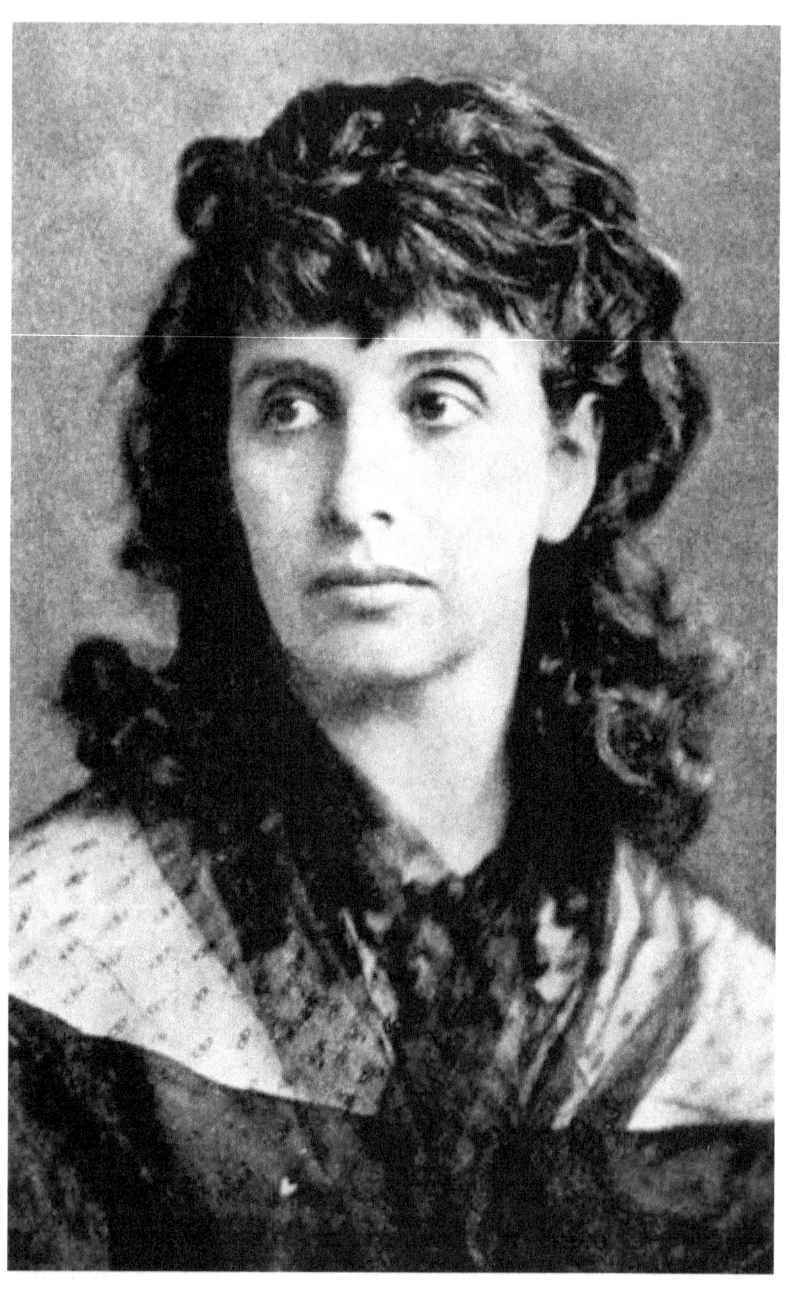

Hedwig Dohm, photograph, ca. 1870
http://www.zeno.org/Literatur/I/dohmhpor

Editor's Introduction

Hedwig Dohm's short story opens with a description of Agnes Schmidt, a mysterious old woman, said to have the eyes of a 'Seherin'. Already within the first paragraph, an English translator encounters a challenge: how do we translate a gendered term (the word *Seherin* is the feminine form of *Seher*) and convey its metaphysical and poetic connotations without falling into clichés? A 'Seher' is a seer, a prophet, someone who sees beyond reality, and here, in Dohm's short story, it is used to describe a woman in a psychiatric institution. This small word announces the main themes of the narrative: how an old woman feels isolated and estranged from society and experiences madness as a kind of metaphysical experience that liberates her from social constraints. The translator will have to tackle the manyfold challenges of this narrative, notably its strategic use of gendered language, its poetic innovations, but also deal with a style that has the potential to sound old-fashioned to a modern reader. They will have to convey the metaphysical meaning of the story of a woman's quest for meaning and for her Self. In several instances, we chose to translate 'mein Ich' by 'my Self' to convey how Agnes deems that society has deprived her of the opportunity to know her true identity – an identity that she is trying to recover through her diary.

All these aspects of Dohm's narrative accompanied us throughout our collaborative translation: how do we translate Dohm's feminist message? How do we convey the poetry of this text, first published in 1894, while making it accessible for English readers in the twenty-first century? This introduction will give readers a glimpse into this narrative, its context, and the challenges we faced, as a group, to translate this short story.

The story opens with a detached narrator describing an old woman, Agnes Schmidt, in a psychiatric institution where she has been brought after a mental breakdown. As she is dying, she gives her diary to her doctor, in the hope that he will understand how she came to lose her sanity. The reader is then offered a direct access to Agnes' thoughts and struggles by reading her diary which she started after the death of her husband. At the beginning of this writing project, Agnes asks herself: 'Something worth recounting in my life? Is there such a thing? And what would it be? I have long been sat here with a pen in my hand trying to recollect it. Nothing, nothing!'. As a widow, Agnes is considered as an outcast in nineteenth-century Germany: as she is no longer of an age to procreate and no longer sexually attractive, her worth as a woman and even as a human being is denied. By granting the type of the 'old woman', rarely featured in Western literature except in comic genres, the opportunity to tell her own story, Dohm deconstructs what has been constructed as 'nothing', as unworthy of being told when it comes to women's lives.

By the time she publishes this short story in 1894, Hedwig Dohm is already famous for her essays and her analyses of the feminine condition. Marianne Adelaide Hedwig Dohm (née Schlesinger) was born in September 1831, the fourth of eighteen children, to the tobacco seller Gustav Schlesinger and Wilhelmine Henriette Jülich. Her father, born Jewish, converted to Protestantism in 1817. She is seventeen when the 1848 revolution breaks out in Germany, a crucial moment in the history of German feminism as more and more women write, publish, and take political action. She receives a limited education before she marries her husband, Ernst, in 1853, the director of the satirical newspaper *Kladderadatsch*. They have four daughters and a son, who dies at eleven years old. The couple frequents the intellectual circles of Berlin and Hedwig Dohm makes her publication debut in the 1870s with *Was die Pastoren von den Frauen denken* (*What Ministers Think about Women*, 1872), a book responding to religious male figures' statements about women. In *Die wissenschaftliche Emancipation der Frauen* (*The Intellectual Emancipation of Women*, 1874), she reflects on women's lack of access to education, a major concern of German feminists at the time. But Dohm is bolder than most of her counterparts: she is one of the first German feminists to demand the right to vote for women. In her essays, she questions what has been constructed as women's 'natural' traits and imagines a more egalitarian future. Her famous quote 'Die Menschenrechte haben kein Geschlecht'[1] (*Human rights don't have a gender*) is inscribed on her grave, in Berlin. Hedwig Dohm dies at the age of 87 on the first of July 1919, a few months after German women voted for the first time in the federal election.

The short story 'Werde, die du bist!' is Dohm's first foray into fiction. It builds an interesting parallel with her later essay *Die Mütter. Ein Betrag zur Erziehungsfrage* (*Mothers. An Essay on the Question of Education*, 1903) in which she ponders on what has been constructed as women's natural role: that of motherhood. In this essay, she argues that women will become better mothers once they are granted more rights. She also discusses the social status of the 'old woman': 'War das Weib untauglich geworden zur Gebärerin, Kinderpflegerin und Geliebten, so hörte ihre Existenzberechtigung auf' (*Once a woman became unfit to be a mother, a caregiver, and a lover, then her right to exist has ceased*).[2] Agnes, in the short story, slowly loses her sanity as she realises her insignificance in the eyes of others. She is mocked, humiliated by family members and strangers, and finally breaks down as she cannot reconcile the split she feels between her external appearance, object of disdain, and her newfound spiritual freedom. By portraying an old woman and making her the object of readers' empathy, Dohm innovates on a literary level as well: the old woman is portrayed as a tragic heroine, on the same level as Shakespeare's King Lear or Balzac's Père Goriot.[3] Despite clear thematic parallels, scholars have underlined the discrepancy between Dohm's essays and their forward-looking optimism and the pessimism of her fiction. 'Werde, die du bist!' portrays the despair of an old woman who is struggling against external judgements which clash with her feelings of being young again now that she is freed from the shackles of marriage and

---

[1] Hedwig Dohm, *Der Frauen Natur und Recht. Zur Frauenfrage zwei Abhandlungen über Eigenschaften und Stimmrecht der Frauen* (Berlin: Wedekind & Schwieger, 1876), p. 184.
[2] Hedwig Dohm, *Die Mütter. Beitrag zur Erziehungsfrage* (Berlin: S. Fischer, 1903), p. 204.
[3] Dohm, *Die Mütter*, p. 206.

motherhood. Agnes slowly loses control over her actions, mind, and speech, leading to her being admitted to a psychiatric institution which appears as a symbol of patriarchal control over any woman considered as deviating from the norm. Agnes' story is the extreme of an old woman's destiny in a patriarchal society that only values women for their external appearance and their fertility, while denying them access to education and creativity. Agnes obsessively ponders over what her life might have been if she had been given the same opportunities as a man: 'What would have become of me? […] Maybe a writer? I see, I sense, I think. I want to create something, craft something from the depths of my chest, where a spring flows free; yet there's no vessel for me to draw from and the bubbling waters are trickling away, they trickle away, taking my life blood with them. I can weep, bitterly, yet I can't describe the tears. What I feel, it's wild like the sea, glittering, vast and deadly. I can't put it into words'. Agnes' tragedy is caused by being born 'too early': 'Being born a hundred years too early, that's it. When my time finally comes, I'll be long gone, dead, decayed'. Agnes is what Dohm has called in some of her other fictional works an 'Übergangsgeschöpf', an individual in a time of transition, in a society that is on the verge of a social revolution. She can feel that women's condition is about to change but that it is too late for her to benefit from this change.

While the story ends tragically with Agnes' definitive silence, there is a glimpse of hope for nineteenth-century as well as for modern readers: by telling this story, by giving a voice to an outcast figure, Dohm invites us to consider how Agnes' tragedy could have been avoided. As Dohm argues in one of her essays, women's tragedy can be overcome by concrete measures: 'Gegen den Tod ist kein Kraut gewachsen; aber gegen den zu frühen Tod des Weibes sind viele Kräutlein gewachsen. Das kräftigste heißt: bedingungslose Emanzipation der Frau und damit die Erlösung von dem brutalen Aberglauben, dass ihr Daseinsrecht nur auf dem Geschlecht beruhe' (*There is no herb that can cure death, but there are many herbs that have grown that can be used against women's premature death. The most powerful is woman's unconditional emancipation and through it the release from the brutal superstition that her right to exist is based only on her sex).*[4] Although social change remains elusive for the fictional character, the narrative of 'Werde, die du bist' is envisioned as precisely such a 'herb': by encouraging the reader to recognise the factors shaping women's lives, Dohm calls for change in the 'real world'.

This short story is also a fascinating insight into a mind's gradual loss of control which introduces notable stylistic innovations: the reader witnesses directly on the page the parallel between Agnes' increasingly fragmented writing and her loss of identity. The rather old-fashioned use of an embedded narrative with the diary also reinforces Dohm's political message and reveals her feminist critique of contemporary realist and naturalist narratives. Instead of having a detached narrator describing the plight of the characters, this story offers a first-person account of Agnes' struggles. The embedded diary is also a direct response to contemporary medical discourses. Dohm questions contemporary definitions of madness that entirely ignore social factors to privilege a biological definition, which posits women as physiologically prone to madness. Agnes deems madness capable of giving her access to a higher realm of reality, reminiscent of the Romantics' idealisation of madness and its association with creative genius.

But the narrative is careful not to overly idealise madness by portraying how Agnes' madness stems from the fact that she is unable to create and struggles to express herself: 'Writing comes naturally to me, as if I've done nothing else since the days of my youth. Ideas, images flood over me in confused abundance. And yet – I also cannot write what I want to write. That's because I don't have half, not even a quarter, of an education. I long for words which aspire to something higher, sentences more finely articulated, they are there in my head – locked up. I shake, shake – alas, the bolt does not budge'. It is her lack of access to creative expression in a society that restricts

---

[4] Dohm, *Die Mütter*, p. 215.

women's destinies to the realm of the household that cause her madness. The internal reader, her doctor, indeed fails to understand where her madness comes from: 'The diary ended here. Doctor Behrend did not find in it what he had hoped to: psychological material on the development of mental illnesses'. The reader is invited to overcome the internal reader's failure to understand the social origins of Agnes' madness. In this story, Dohm gestures at a modern and political conception of madness by portraying it as the female character's lack of access to education, creative expression, and opportunities for growth.

Dohm indeed ironically uses a positive title, the Pindaric motto of 'Become who you are', quoted by Friedrich Nietzsche in *Also sprach Zarathustra* (1883) as 'Werde, der du bist'. Despite her struggle, Agnes simply cannot recover her identity after years of fulfilling her expected role as a daughter, wife, and mother, thus failing to correspond to Pindar's ideal. We decided to translate this title as 'The Woman You Become' because Dohm consciously changes the male pronoun 'der' into 'die', challenging the use of the masculine as universal in German. Our translated title can also be read as a reference to the French feminist, Simone de Beauvoir, and her famous statement: 'One is not born, but rather, becomes a woman'.[5] Both feminists indeed reject biological definitions of womanhood to rather focus on how it has been socially constructed, showing that, although they are forgotten, there are clear links between nineteenth-century feminism and our modern feminist thinking. 'The Woman You Become' also refers to the potential optimism which can be found in this story: the reader is supposed to recognise that the shackles – 'thin as cobwebs' – that entrap Agnes can be broken.

Marie Martine
Oxford, June 2025

---

[5] Simone de Beauvoir, *The Second Sex*, translated by Constance Borde and Sheila Malovany-Chevalier (London: Vintage Books, 2011), p. 146. [1949]

Translators' Introduction

The introduction is composed of the individual reflections by the four translators as mosaic pieces, signed off collectively.

Translating a text written and set in late 19th century Germany for a 21st century English-speaking audience presents many challenges, especially given the feminist nature and poetic quality of Dohm's original work. The short story opens with 'In der Irrenanstalt des Doktor Behrend', which we have translated as 'In Doctor Behrend's asylum'. The key word to consider here was 'Irrenanstalt', a compound literally denoting an 'institution for mad-people'. This noun is flagged as archaic and discriminatory by Duden, due to its reliance on outdated stereotypes of mental illness; the adjective form, 'irre', is even accompanied by a warning that this word is no longer acceptable in public discourse, with more neutral or technical terms such as 'geistig / psychisch behindert' (mentally/psychologically disabled) suggested as alternatives. Whilst the pejorative force of 'Irrenanstalt' could have been conveyed with English equivalents such as 'madhouse' or 'loony bin', the decision to include these similarly problematic terms in our translation would arguably act to promote the very discourse around mental illnesses which Dohm aims to criticize through her sympathetic portrayal of Agnes. The use of more neutral terms, such as 'asylum' for 'Irrenanstalt', and 'psychiatrist' for 'Irrenarzt' (mad-doctor), therefore felt more compatible with our feminist project; these alternatives were used at the time at which Dohm was writing, allowing us to avoid perpetuating the misogynistic discourse around madness and hysteria without being anachronistic.

At other points in the text, we have chosen to preserve and even enhance the pejorative force of the original, in order to create an equivalent effect for a modern English reader. For example, Agnes is twice described as 'Sappho aus den Fliegenden Blättern' ('Sappho from the Flying Leaves'). Here, Dohm makes reference to a German satirical journal, *Die Fliegenden Blätter* (1844-1928), which published comics, poems, and short stories on a weekly basis, and would likely have been familiar to Dohm's contemporaries. To modern English readers, however, the effect of this allusion is better conveyed by making the implication more explicit: Agnes, like the humorous caricatures of the *Fliegende Blätter*, is being mocked as 'a grotesque Sappho'.

Other instances of irony risk being obscured due to language difference. This is especially significant for words describing women and mothers, a lexical field notorious for its liability to pejoration; because of this, both English and German have a plethora of ostensibly identical terms for women which can nonetheless differ greatly in their connotations. As part of her feminist project, Dohm addresses how women are affected by the negative connotations which tend to accumulate to words with female referents. Agnes discusses the variety of names which she is called by her daughters' families ('Mämmchen', 'Mutter', 'Mamachen', 'Mama'), lamenting that her identity is reduced to these diminutive and overly-familiar forms. We chose to retain these German words in our translation, as such linguistic metadiscourse lends itself to having the source language visible to the reader; furthermore, it would be difficult to translate the formal and semantic variety of these largely synonymous terms without losing some nuances of the original.

As a German author, Dohm is also able to utilise grammatical gender to explore how women are marginalised through language. Agnes writes in her diary that '*Der* Alte ist eine liebenswürdige Vorstellung, *die* Alte eine unangenehme.' ('The old *man* is an agreeable image, the old *woman* is a repulsive one'). In the first edition, the gendered articles 'der' and 'die', in 'Sperrsatz' (spaced-out lettering) for added emphasis (rendered in our edition as *italics*), effectively highlight how the same noun ('Alte') can take on opposite connotations based on whether it has a masculine or feminine referent; in English, we chose to convey this by creating a similar parallelism between the noun phrases 'old *man*' and 'old *woman*'. Gendered language is also brought into focus at the end of this passage, as Agnes comments on how the phrase 'altes Weib' ('old woman') is the perceived as the ultimate insult. The term 'Weib' carries increasingly misogynistic connotations in modern German, with possible English translations being 'wench', 'hag', or even 'broad'. Whilst the phrase is indeed intended to be offensive in this context, Agnes / Dohm is using this to highlight how the fundamentally neutral traits of being old and female are perceived so negatively by society that simply describing them can function as an insult. We therefore opted for the more neutral translation of 'old lady' to allow this feminist critique to shine through, as well as to avoid the use of misogynistic terms in our own translation.

* * *

Not unlike Agnes herself, we too formed an affiliation with the natural world presented by Dohm. Upon reading the novella for the first time, we were struck by the vivacious omnipresence of botanical and floral imagery which enriches the text. Since the human female genealogy of which Agnes is a part is stifled by the control imposed on it by the men around her, namely her sons-in-law who attempt to manage her relationships with both her children and grandchildren, she seeks this connection elsewhere – in nature. Throughout the text, the natural world is presented as a feminine realm, abundant with flowers, vines, plants, and water, and it is here that Agnes can truly thrive as a most unapologetic Self. So profound is this connection that the natural world appears to form a symbiotic relationship with the protagonist, taking on an animate life of its own as a sort of personified companion to the otherwise lonely and isolated widow, accompanying her wherever she goes. This personification is largely achieved through an adoption of humane qualifiers and verbs, all of which we strove to replicate in translation. However, it also shines through in the inherently female gender of the German noun: die Natur. Thanks to the gendered system of the German language, the very grammar allows for a female genealogy to be formed between Agnes and the natural world, substituting that which she lacks with her mortal relatives. However, since English grammar does not function in the same gendered manner, it is incapable of replicating this precisely. Thus, upon translating the noun into English, we lost part of its significance. For this reason, we resolved to gender nature deliberately in our translation, despite this not being the immediate choice, occasionally translating 'die Natur' as 'Mother Nature' where it should be 'nature' and substituting the neutral pronoun 'it' for 'she/her'.

The integrity of the natural world – or Mother Nature – to the text and to the characterisation of the protagonist was also a deciding factor in the illustrations used for both the front cover and in-text drawings. One particular motif which resonated with us when translating the text was the headless statue found by Agnes in the Tiergarten which, as we translate, is 'mottled all over with red, as though blood were dripping from the headless trunk, making the roses blaze so red'. Together with the myrtle wreath which Agnes (quite literally) lives and dies in, the symbol of the head and theme of headlessness are also of utmost importance. The lost head of the statue, which comes to mimic Agnes' own 'headlessness' in the eyes of the society around her, is seen again in the lake on Capri and later returned to in Agnes' very last utterances. Although both this headless statue and motif of the flower might traditionally be considered a feminine marker of fragility and weakness, Dohm uses the first-person, agent voice of Agnes to reassign these to both the protagonist and, by extension, women of her time and age, allowing them to reclaim them as symbols of female strength.

* * *

Translating as a group is no mean feat, even less so when the group consists of four strong-willed and grammar-obsessed students. Beginning in Hilary, each week we offered up our translated sections, ready to accept and, as our confidence (and stubbornness) grew, fiercely defend our suggestions. From debates over the difference between myself, my self and my Self (very different, trust us) to the age-old question, to capitalise, or not to capitalise? We spent countless hours in locations around Queen's from the tiny window seat in Marie's office to outside on the lawn in Drawda discussing and editing the previous week's work.

Our primary focus as a group was preserving the feminist message and tone of the text. We did so by using feminist translation strategies to create an end product faithful to Dohm, ourselves, and perhaps most crucially, to Agnes. One recurring point of discussion was the use of footnotes, often employed by feminist translators to explain additions or substitutions in cases of gendering lost between languages. After many weeks of deliberation, we opted for minimal footnotes, explaining culturally specific references in order to keep the text accessible. Women spend their lives having to justify and explain their decisions, why should this transfer into our work?

We also had to reckon with some of the more uncomfortable parts of the original language. One term in particular, 'Zigeuner', now considered a slur, posed a particular challenge. In the end, we chose to leave it in the original German rather than translate it, as its equivalent 'Gypsy,' carries its own problematic weight in English. We considered alternatives like 'Sinti' or 'Roma,' but felt that naming specific groups risked being more exclusionary than accurate. By keeping 'Zigeuner' we were able to highlight the problematic usage without perpetuating it.

Naturally, not every decision we made was quite so weighty. Between the moments of real linguistic reckoning, there were plenty of debates driven more by tone, rhythm, and 'vibes'. Translation of this nature, we found, lives somewhere between fidelity and flair, and sometimes, flair wins. Over the past few months my own rather less conscious focus then became, 'how ridiculous can my typos end up?' German is a marvellous language, in which the absence or addition of a single letter can change the meaning of a word entirely. This became a true source of entertainment for the group, as by week 4, when our workload had doubled in order to reach the printing deadline, I had decided that 'meines Lieblingsfelsens' and 'meines

Lieblingsfehlens' were indeed interchangeable. Turns out that when Agnes gets up from the table she does not 'hurry as fast as I can to the lonely height of my favourite mistake' but to the 'lonely height of my favourite cliff.' Philosophical? Yes. Accurate? Apparently not. The group had spoken – cliff it was.

Translating this text with three of my best friends has been a total joy. I'm eternally grateful for their patience, intelligence, and wit, and will never forget their laughter when I decided that 'fernsehend' meant 'television-seeking' rather than 'far-seeing', – tricky, considering the television didn't yet exist in 1894. I have learnt so much from them, and this experience will be one I will never forget. To Marie, without whom this entire project wouldn't even exist, thank you. You have changed the way we look at translation, and the completion of this work is down to your dedication and generosity. To finish, here's to Hedwig Dohm herself, who no doubt would have had plenty to say about our translation choices, we only hope we've made you proud.

Emily Dicker, Victoria Mckinley-Smith,
Lia Neill, and Isabella Reese
Oxford, June 2025

Hedwig Dohm.

Wie Frauen werden.   Werde, die Du bist.

Title-page of the first edition of the collection of novellas
Copy of the Bayerische Staatsbibliothek München, P.o.germ. 1788 o

Hedwig Dohm
Edition and Translation

The edition is based on the open access version https://www.projekt-gutenberg.org/autoren/namen/dohm.html which in turn follows the first edition published in Wroclaw by the *Schlesische Buchdruckerei, Kunst- und Verlags-Anstalt S. Schottlaender* in 1894, where it was linked with another novella under the combined title 'Wie Frauen werden. – Werde, die Du bist. Novellen von Hedwig Dohm', pp. 149–236, online accessible via the Bayerische Staatsbibliothek https://www.digitale-sammlungen.de/de/view/bsb11674964. A version with the original spelling is available via zeno.org.

The spelling of the German text which Projekt Gutenberg had slightly modernized has been further adjusted to modern German spelling. The title itself ends with an exclamation mark on the first page of the novella but with a full stop on the frontpage of the book, probably because the large Gothic font did not have exclamation marks. The original paragraph structure is maintained, as are the sections formed by three asterisks * * *. For major caesuras, they have been replaced in the translation by the rose symbols designed for this edition. Phrases highlighted by s p a c i n g in the original have been marked by *italics*.

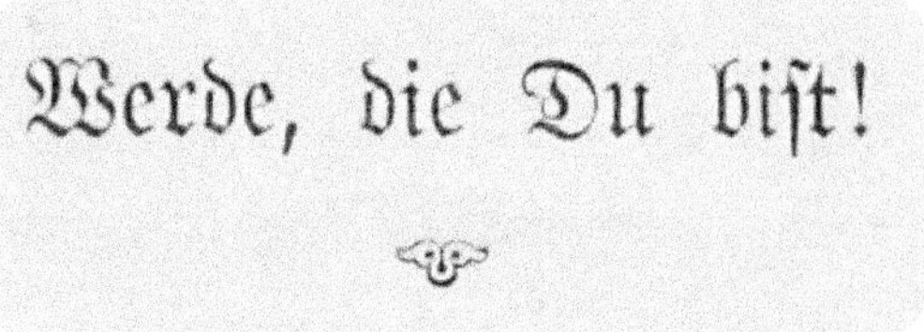

Title-page of the novella in the first edition
Copy of the Bayerische Staatsbibliothek München, P.o.germ. 1788 o

Werde, die du bist!

In der Irrenanstalt des Doktor Behrend, in der Nähe Berlins, machte eine alte Frau – sie mochte nah an sechzig sein – Aufsehen. Sie hatte feine, interessante Gesichtszüge, starkes graues Haar und große grünlich graue Augen. Niemals starrten diese Augen in's Leere. Entweder schienen sie, erloschen für Außenwelt, innerlich etwas zu schauen, oder sie waren emporgerichtet, bald mit dem Ausdruck eines leidenschaftlichen, irrenden Suchens, bald mit Entzücken sich an einen Gegenstand festsaugend. Die Augen einer Seherin. Diese wundersamen Augen geben dem Kopf den Charakter einer jüngeren Frau.

Sie verhielt sich meist schweigsam. Zuweilen aber fing sie an zu reden, dann war es, als hielte sie Zwiesprache mit übernatürlichen Wesen. Unermessliche Melancholie oder dithyrambische Verzückung atmeten ihre Worte. Sie sprach tiefsinnige und erhabene Gedanken aus, in einer Form, die an Nietzsches Zarathustra erinnerte.

Man hätte glauben sollen, dass diese alte Frau eine große Dichterin gewesen und dass ein Übermaß geistiger Erregung die Gehirnstörung bewirkt habe. Das Gegenteil war der Fall.

Der Nervenarzt, der sich für diese merkwürdige Form von Irrsinn interessierte, zog Erkundigungen über ihr Vorleben ein. Was er erfuhr, setzte ihn in das höchste Erstaunen und war in keiner Weise angetan, das Rätsel ihres Wesens zu lösen.

The Woman You Become

In Doctor Behrend's asylum near Berlin, an old woman – she must have been about sixty – was causing a stir. She had delicate, attractive features, thick grey hair, and big greenish-grey eyes. Eyes which never stared into space. They either seemed to turn their gaze inwards, detached from the outside world, or were directed upwards as if on an impassioned yet vagrant quest, when not eagerly attached to some object. The eyes of a prophetess. Wondrous eyes which gave her the appearance of a young woman.

Most of the time, she remained silent. Occasionally, however, she began to speak, and then it was as if she were in conversation with otherworldly beings. Her words breathed with unfathomable melancholy and unrestrained ecstasy. She uttered profound, sublime thoughts in a way which recalled Nietzsche's Zarathustra.[1]

It would be easy to believe that this woman had been a great poet, and that an excess of intellectual stimulation had led to her mental disorder. It was in fact the opposite.

The psychiatrist interested in this peculiar kind of insanity had asked what her life had been like before. His findings left him in the utmost astonishment, not in the least bit helping him to crack her puzzling nature.

---

[1] This is a reference to the book by the German philosopher Friedrich Nietzsche, *Thus Spoke Zarathustra* (1883–1885). The character of Zarathustra discusses central concepts of Nietzsche's philosophy, including the 'Übermensch', the death of God, and the eternal recurrence.

Alle, die die Gattin des Geheimen Kanzleirats Schmidt gekannt, stimmten darin überein, dass sie eine gute, brave, etwas beschränkte und philiströse Hausfrau gewesen, unwissend und völlig im Familienleben aufgehend. Sie hatte zwei Töchter, die längst verheiratet waren. Ihr Verhältnis zu den Kindern war jederzeit ein überaus herzliches gewesen. In den letzten acht Jahren hatte sie in aufopfernder Weise ihren gelähmten Mann gepflegt. Nach seinem Tode mochte sie sich etwas vereinsamt gefühlt haben. Sie war zum Besuch bei ihren verheirateten Töchtern gewesen. Keiner der Anverwandten hatte die geringste Exzentrizität an ihr bemerkt, nur war sie ihnen etwas schweigsamer und in sich gekehrter als sonst vorgekommen, was in der Trauer um den Gatten und in ihrer Vereinsamung eine ausreichende Erklärung fand.

Dann hatte sie allerdings, ziemlich plötzlich, und von ihren Töchtern missbilligt, ganz allein größere Reisen unternommen, trotz ihrer beschränkten Mittel. Bald nach ihrer Rückkehr war der Irrsinn zum Ausbruch gekommen.

Die Kranke nahm wenig Nahrung zu sich, sie magerte zusehends ab, so dass schließlich die großen flimmernden Augen in dem bleichen Gesicht unheimlich wirkten. Es war, als wenn die Seele allmählich den Leib verzehrte, verzehren wollte.

Eigentümlich war, dass diese alte Frau mit einer gewissen Zärtlichkeit an dem Kostüm hing, das sie trug, als man sie in die Anstalt brachte: Ein schwarz wollenes Kleid, das den Schnitt aus dem Zeitalter Marie Antoinettes hatte. Das volle graue Haar, an den Spitzen leicht gelockt, fiel ihr fast bis auf die Schulter. Im Laufe der zwei Jahre, die sie in der Anstalt zubrachte, war es weiß geworden. Alls man ihr das Haar aufstecken wollte, litt sie es nicht. Dasselbe geschah, als man ihr für das abgetragene Kleid ein neues, von anderem Schnitt reichte. Sie war nicht zu bewegen es anzuziehen. Man musste ihr ein Kostüm genau nach dem Schnitt des alten anfertigen lassen.

Everyone who knew Privy Councillor Schmidt's wife agreed that she was a good and honest housewife, if somewhat prim and narrow-minded, ignorant and unquestioningly committed to domestic life. She had two daughters, both of whom had married long ago. She had always had a highly cordial relationship with her children. During the last eight years of her marriage, she had cared for her bedridden husband in a self-sacrificing manner. After his death she might have felt somewhat lonely. She had paid visits to her married daughters. No one among her relatives had noticed in her even the slightest eccentricity, she seemed to them only somewhat quieter and more withdrawn than usual, which was readily explained by the grief for her husband and her loneliness.

Then, however – quite suddenly and much to her daughters' disapproval – she was setting off on great travels entirely independently, in spite of her limited means. Soon after her return, the insanity came to a head.

The patient took little food, she visibly wasted away, to the extent that, eventually, the great glimmering eyes in the pale face seemed uncanny. It was as though the soul was gradually consuming the body, or attempting to.

It was an idiosyncrasy of hers that the old woman hung on with a certain tenderness to the clothing she was wearing when she was brought to the institution: a black woollen dress cut from a pattern belonging to Marie Antoinette's era. Her thick, grey hair, curling slightly at the ends, fell almost to her shoulders. In the course of the two years which she spent in the institution, it had become white. She would not tolerate attempts to put her hair up. The same happened when she was offered, in place of the worn-out dress, a new, differently cut one. She could not be convinced to wear it. A dress had to be made exactly to the pattern of the old one.

Man hatte beobachtet, dass sie allsonntäglich, wenn in der kleinen Kapelle die Orgel zu spielen begann, einen welken Myrtenkranz aus ihrer Kommode nahm; der Arzt vermutete, ihren Brautkranz. Sie schmückte sich mit dem Kranz und blieb, die Hände gegen die Brust gedrückt, die Augen mit einem gespannten Ausdruck auf die Tür gerichtet, mitten im Zimmer stehen, bis die Orgel verklang. Dann legte sie, den Kopf leise schüttelnd, den Kranz zurück; verhüllte ihr Gesicht mit einem schwarzen Schleier und nahm den ganzen Tag über keine Speise zu sich.

Einige Male war sie von ihren Töchtern besucht worden. Sei waren beim Anblick der Mutter ebenso verwundert wie betrübt gewesen. Sowohl im Ausdruck als in den Zügen fanden sie sie völlig verändert und vermochten kaum sich in eine kindliche Beziehung zu dieser fremdartigen Erscheinung hinein zu denken.

Die Kranke, als sie ihre Töchter sah, schien sich auf etwas zu besinnen. Allmählich geriet sie in eine Unruhe, die sich so steigerte, dass der Arzt den Besuch abkürzen musste. Als die Töchter ein zweites Mal kamen und sich dieselbe Erregung bei ihr kund gab, bat er die jungen Frauen, ihre Besuche für einige Zeit einzustellen, entließ sie aber mit der Hoffnung für die Wiederherstellung der Mutter.

Seit zwei Jahren nun beobachtete Doktor Behrend, im Interesse der psychologischen Wissenschaft, mit intensiver Spannung dieses seltene Beispiel eines gestörten Geistes, bei dem die Störung gewissermaßen ein neues Individuum geschaffen hatte. Sie fühlte das Interesse, das er an ihr nahm, und oft heftete sie ihre Augen minutenlang auf ihn, wie mit einer forschenden Frage, einem düster schmerzlichen Erstaunen.

Eines Tages kam ein junger, süddeutscher Arzt, ein Studiengenosse des Irrenarztes, in die Anstalt, um dieselbe zu besichtigen. Doktor Behrend erzählte ihm von seinem interessanten Fall und willfahrte gern dem Kollegen, als dieser den Wunsch aussprach, die Patientin zu sehen.

It had been observed that, whenever the organ began to play in the small chapel, she took a wilted myrtle wreath out of her chest of drawers; the doctor surmised that it was her bridal wreath. She adorned herself with it and remained standing in the middle of the room, her hands pressed against her chest, her eyes fixed in a tense expression towards the door, until the organ died away. Then she put the wreath back, shaking her head gently, covered her face with a black veil and did not eat a thing for the rest of the day.

Her daughters had visited a few times. They had been both astonished and saddened at the sight of their mother. They found her completely changed, in both her expression and in her features, and could hardly imagine a familial relationship with this strange apparition.

The patient, when she saw her daughters, seemed to have something on her mind. Gradually she became so agitated that the doctor had to cut the visit short. When her daughters visited a second time and provoked the same reaction, he asked the young women to pause their visits for some time, but left them with the hope of their mother's recovery.

For two years now, Doctor Behrend, in the interest of psychological science, had been observing with intense curiosity this strange example of a troubled mind, within which the disturbance had created a new individual. She felt the interest that he took in her and her eyes often rested on him for minutes at a time, as if with an enquiring question, a dull, painful astonishment.

One day a young, south-German doctor, who had studied alongside the psychiatrist, came to visit the asylum. Doctor Behrend had told him about his interesting case, and happily obliged his colleague when he expressed his desire to see the patient.

Gerade an dem Tage – es war ein Sonntag – vollendete die Kranke ihr sechzigstes Lebensjahr. Die Töchter hatten Blumen geschickt, das ganze Zimmer duftete davon.

Als die beiden Ärzte eintraten, war sie dabei, die Blumen über den Fußboden hinzustreuen. In das weiße Haar hatte sie den verdorrten Myrtenkranz gedrückt. Mit den spitzen bräunlichen Stielen und den welken Blättchen, zwischen denen nur hier und da noch ein paar tote vergilbte Blüten schwankten, glich er einer Dornenkrone. In der Hand hielt sie eine vertrocknete Passionsblume.

Und nun geschah etwas völlig Unerwartetes. Als die Greisin den fremden Arzt erblickte, überzog eine tiefe Röte ihr Gesicht. In ihre schattenhafte Erscheinung kam pulsierendes Leben, in ihre Augen flackerndes Licht.

"Johannes!" und sie streckte dem Fremden beide Hände entgegen. Ihre Stimme klang weich und voll.

"Ich wusste, dass Du kommen würdest. Wenn ich Deine Myrte trage, sehe ich in die Ferne."

Sie berührte mit der Hand den welken Kranz. "An jenem Tag, als Du mir die Myrte gabst, hast Du Dich mir verlobt. Komm! Komm! Die weiße Opferflamme brennt in der güldenen Schale, Du weißt, in der Höhle auf Capri. Wir dürfen ihn nicht warten lassen, den Silberhaarigen. Hörst Du das metallne Singen aus der Tiefe? Die Sirenen! Das blaue Meer, sie tragen's als Juwel an der Brust. Sie singen mit blutroten Lippen. Sie singen das Brautlied. Und ich küsse Deine Seele."

Die letzten Worte hatte sie halbsingend gesprochen. Sie küsste die welke Blume in ihrer Hand, und langsam, ohne ihn anzusehen, schritt sie auf ihn zu.

On that very day – it was a Sunday – the patient was reaching the end of her sixtieth year of life. Her daughters had sent flowers; their smell filled the entire room.

As the two doctors entered, she was scattering the flowers across the floor. She had pinned the withered myrtle wreath into her white hair. With its spiky brown stalks and limp leaves, interspersed with a few dead, yellowed blossoms swaying here and there, it resembled a crown of thorns. In her hand she held a shrivelled passionflower.

And then, something completely unexpected happened. When the old woman saw the young doctor, a deep redness flushed over her face. Into her shadowy appearance came pulsing life, into her eyes, flickering light.

'Johannes!' – and she stretched both hands towards the stranger. Her voice was tender and full.

'I knew that you would come. Whenever I wear your myrtle, I see you in the distance.'

She stroked the wilted wreath with her hand. 'On the day when you gave me the myrtle, you betrothed yourself to me. Come! Come! The white sacrificial flame is burning in the golden cup, you know, in the cave in Capri. We cannot afford to keep him waiting, the silver-haired one. Do you hear the metal singing from the deep? The sirens! The blue sea, they wear it like a jewel on their chests. They sing with blood-red lips. They sing the bridal song. And I kiss your soul.'

She was half-singing as she uttered those last words. She kissed the wilted flowers in her hand and slowly, without looking up, moved towards him.

Doktor Behrend, peinlich von der Szene berührt, und in der Besorgnis, dass etwas Ungehöriges geschehen könne, ergriff die Irre am Arm und sagte hart und laut, wie er sonst nie zu ihr sprach:

"Besinnen Sie sich, Frau Schmidt, vergessen Sie nicht, dass Sie eine alte Dame sind."

Die Kranke schauderte und sah erst ihn, dann den fremden Arzt an. Eine unheimliche Veränderung ging in ihrem Gesicht vor. Fluchtartig irrten die Augensterne in ihren Kreisen. Allmählich schienen die Züge zu erstarren. Wie ein brennendes Scheit, das plötzlich in sich zusammen sinkt und Asche wird, so brach ihr Körper zusammen. Sie wäre zu Boden gestürzt, wenn Doktor Behrend sie nicht in seinen Armen aufgefangen hätte. Eine tiefe Ohnmacht umfing sie.

Man brachte sie zu Bett. Als die Ohnmacht in Schlaf übergegangen war, kehrte Doktor Behrend zu seinem Kollegen zurück. Er versicherte ihm, dass die Kranke noch niemals einen ähnlichen Unfall gehabt. Von erotischem Wahnsinn habe sich bisher bei ihr keine Spur gezeigt. Er würde annehmen, dass sie den Kollegen mit ihrem verstorbenen Gatten identifiziert, aber dieser habe Eduard geheißen.

"Und ich heiße Johannes," entgegnete der Fremde in trüber Verstimmung.

"Höchst sonderbar! Und dass sie sich einbildete, Sie zu kennen."

"Sie kennt mich. Ich traf sie vor drei Jahren auf Capri. Mir fiel damals ihre eigentümliche Erscheinung auf. Sie trug dasselbe Kleid, oder ein ähnliches wie heut."

Ob er näher mit ihr bekannt geworden, forschte Doktor Behrend.

Doctor Behrend, deeply embarrassed by the scene in front of him and afraid that something improper might occur, seized the insane woman by the arm, and said in a loud, harsh tone, unlike he had ever used on her before:

'Control yourself, Mrs Schmidt. Don't forget that you are an old lady.'

The patient shuddered, looking first at him and then at the visiting doctor. An unsettling transformation took place in her face. Her pupils darted about in their orbs. Gradually, her features seemed to freeze in place. Just like a smouldering log collapses and turns to ash, her body caved in on itself. She would have fallen to the floor if Doctor Behrend had not caught her in his arms. Intense weakness made her faint.

She was put to bed. When the faintness had passed into sleep, Doctor Behrend turned back to his colleague, assuring him that the patient had never had an attack of this kind before. Nor had a single trace of erotic insanity appeared within her until now. He assumed that she saw a resemblance between the doctor and her dead husband, but the latter's name had been Eduard.

'And mine's Johannes,' the visitor replied with a vague tone of discontent.

'Most peculiar! And to think she thought she knew you…'

'She does know me. I came across her three years ago, in Capri. I noticed her peculiar appearance back then. She was wearing the same dress as she is today, or a similar one at least.'

Docter Behrend inquired whether he had become any closer acquainted with her.

Durchaus nicht. Er erinnere sich nicht, mit ihr gesprochen zu haben. Obgleich sie im Hotel Pagano ihm gegenüber gesessen, habe sie sich nie in die Unterhaltung gemischt, doch sei es ihm vorgekommen, als ob sie aufmerksam auf Alles, was er getan und gesprochen, geachtet habe. Wenn er ihr aber auf Spaziergängen begegnet, so sei sie ihm ausgewichen.

Doktor Behrend hat ihn, Alles mitzuteilen, was er über sie in Erfahrung gebracht.

"Es ist nicht viel," antwortete der junge Arzt etwas zögernd.

"Sie hatte ein scheues Wesen, als ob sie um Entschuldigung bäte, dass sie überhaupt da sei. Merkwürdig war, wie verschieden sie aussehen konnte, bald wie eine Greisin, und dann wieder schien sie eine kaum Vierzigjährige.

Einmal traf ich sie unten am Meer, an der kleinen Marine. Sie hatte ihren jungen Tag. Sie bückte sich hinab zum Wasser und murmelte mit lächelnden Lippen vor sich hin. Da sah sie mich und wurde rot wie vorhin. Ich habe immer ein peinliches Gefühl, wenn ich eine alte Frau erröten sehe. Ich wollte sie ansprechen und bemerkte zu meinem Erstaunen, dass sie plötzlich ganz alt und hinfällig wurde. Fremd, fast böse, blickte sie und wandte sich mit einer zuckenden Bewegung der Arme ab. Sie wollte augenscheinlich nicht gestört werden, und so ging ich weiter.

Ein ander Mal bemerkte ich sie auf einem der Felsen, die aus dem Meer emporragen, nicht eben hoch. Sie stand hoch aufgerichtet, mit den Armen nach hinten das Felsstück umklammernd. Ihre Blicke schweiften über das Meer, mit dem Ausdruck, den Menschen haben, die mit der Welt fertig sind, und die auf dem Sprung stehen, eine andere aufzusuchen. Ich blieb stehen, in einer Art Bangigkeit, sie könne sich hinabstürzen wollen. Ich hielt sie für eine Dichterin, die incognito bleiben wollte.

By no means. He didn't remember ever having spoken with her. Although she sat opposite him in the Hotel Pagano, she never took part in conversation, yet it seemed to him as though she was attentive to everything that he did and said. But whenever he came across her on his walks, she avoided him.

Doctor Behrend asked him to detail everything that he had discovered about her.

'There isn't much to tell,' the young doctor answered somewhat hesitantly.

'She had a shy disposition, as though she were apologising simply for being there. It was remarkable how varied her appearance could be, at times she looked like an old woman and then at others she seemed hardly forty years old.

Once I met her down by the sea, at the little marina. She was having one of her youthful days. She was bending down towards the water and murmuring to herself with smiling lips. Then she saw me and went red, like she did just now. I always feel mortified when I see an old woman blush. I was about to speak to her when I noticed, to my astonishment, that she had suddenly become entirely old and decrepit. She glanced at me strangely, almost viciously and then turned away with a twitching movement in her arms. She clearly didn't want to be disturbed, so I walked on.

Another time I noticed her on one of the rocks, not very high, which jutted out from the sea. She stood upright, clutching the rock with her arms behind her. Her eyes wandered over the sea, with the expression of someone finished with this world and one step away from seeking out another. I stopped, worried that she might want to throw herself down into the water. I thought she might be a poet who wanted to remain incognito.

Mir kam der Einfall, ihr irgend eine Art Huldigung darzubringen. Sacht stieg ich hinter ihr an dem Felsen empor und warf ihr einen Myrtenstrauß, den ich frisch gepflückt hatte, vor die Füße. Sie schien nicht verwundert und blickte sich nicht um, lächelte nur und drückte den Strauß an ihre Brust. Sie hatte in diesem Augenblick die Physiognomie eines jungen Mädchens, und ich bedauerte lebhaft, dass sie keins war.

Der Zufall ist zuweilen grausam. Als ich später in den Vorraum des Speisesaales trat, wo sich die Gäste zu versammeln pflegen, näherte sich mir mein Tischnachbar, ein Herr, der für witzig galt, und fragte mich, ob ich vorhin unser vis-à-vis auf dem Felsen bemerkt hätte, die "reine Sappho aus den Fliegenden Blättern". In einer Anwandlung jener niedrigen Feigheit, die uns zuweilen gegen bessere Einsicht zum Echo fremder Lieblosigkeit macht, antwortete ich: "Ja, ich habe 'die Großmutter Psyche' gesehen." Kaum war mir der hässliche Spott entschlüpft, so beschlich mich die unheimliche Empfindung, als stände sie hinter uns. Und sie stand hinter uns. Sie erinnerte mich in jenem Augenblick mit den geöffneten Lippen und den großen, starren und entsetzten Augen an eine Medusa. Wie geistesabwesend trat sie einen Schritt zu mir heran, griff mit einer mechanischen Bewegung nach der Passionsblume, die ich in der Hand hielt, und ging hinaus. Ich war fest entschlossen, auf irgend eine Art gut zu machen, was ich gefrevelt. Es war mir nicht vergönnt. Ich sah sie nicht wieder. Am andern Morgen war sie abgereist. Und dass ich sie nun hier wiederfinde, peinlich ist es für mich, sehr peinlich."

"Es trifft Sie kein Vorwurf," beschwichtigte ihn Doktor Behrend, und mit einem leichten Achselzucken setzte er hinzu: "Anachronismus des Herzens. Nichts Seltenes bei bejahrten Frauen mit allzu sensiblem Nervensystem."

Der Fremde verließ die Anstalt, nachdem er den Irrenarzt gebeten, ihn von dem ferneren Schicksal der Greisin in Kenntnis zu setzen.

It occurred to me to pay her a kind of homage of my own. So I climbed up the rock behind her and threw a myrtle wreath at her feet, which I had freshly picked. She seemed unphased, not even looking around. She just laughed and pressed the branch to her breast. In this moment she had the air of a young girl, and I deeply regretted that she was not in fact one.

Chance is cruel sometimes. Later, as I stepped into the anteroom of the dining room where the guests tended to gather, the person sat next to me, a gentleman who was known for his humour, approached me and asked me if I had noticed our tablemate on the rock earlier, the 'grotesque Sappho.' In a fit of cowardice, which sometimes makes us echo other people's unkindness despite our better judgement, I replied: 'Yes, I have seen Grandma Psyche.' No sooner had the ugly mockery slipped from my lips, I was overcome by the uncanny feeling that she was standing behind us, and indeed she was. In that moment, she reminded me of a Medusa with her open lips and large, glassy and horrifying eyes. As if absent-mindedly, she took a step towards me, reached mechanically for the passionflower which I held in my hand, and went out. I was determined to atone in some way for what I had done. But the opportunity was not granted to me. I never saw her again. The next morning, she had departed. And to find her here again now is embarrassing for me, very embarrassing.'

'You are not to be blamed,' Doctor Behrend assured him, and with a gentle shrug of his shoulders added: 'Anachronism of the heart. Not uncommon amongst elderly women with an overly sensitive nervous system.'

The stranger left the institution, having requested that the psychiatrist inform him of the old woman's eventual fate.

Als Doktor Behrend die Kranke wieder aufsuchte, war sie erwacht. Sie hatte die Fenster weit öffnen lassen. Sie bedeutete die Wärterin, sie mit dem Arzt allein zu lassen. Sie atmete langsam und tief, als tränke sie lebensgierig mit intensivem Bewusstsein die letzten Tropfen aus dem Becher der Zeit. Ihre Nasenflügel zitterten leise. Das Gesicht war ganz durchgeistigt, jede Falte war daraus verschwunden, wie es sonst erst nach dem Tode zu geschehen pflegt.

Noch ehe sie sprach, wusste der Arzt, dass ihr Geist wieder gesund war. Sie reichte ihm die durchsichtige Hand. "Ich danke Ihnen für all Ihre Sorgfalt und Teilnahme, und dass Sie mich still haben gewähren lassen. Hier in Ihrer Anstalt war ich weniger irre als während meines ganzen früheren Lebens. Großes habe ich gedacht, Herrliches geschaut. Träume und Visionen sind ja auch Leben. Wie dem Siegfried ward mir der Vögel Sprache kund."

Sie zeigte auf ein Buch, das auf ihrer Kommode lag. Er brachte es ihr.

"Ich habe nach dem Tode meines Mannes angefangen, ein Tagebuch zu schreiben. Ich bitte Sie, es zu verbrennen. Sie sind Psychologe. Möchten Sie erfahren, wie und warum mein Geist gestört wurde, so lesen Sie es, bevor Sie es vernichten. Niemand sonst soll es lesen."

Er nahm das Buch aus ihrer Hand.

"Ich möchte nicht begraben sein," sagte sie nach einer Pause. "Verbrannt. In Flammen emporlodern – in Flammen! Das will ich."

Und wieder nach einer Pause: "Viele Frauen sterben am Kreuz, ob nur um tot zu sein, wie der arme Schächer, ob für die Andern, wie unser Heiland?"

When Doctor Behrend checked up on the patient again, she had woken up. The windows had been left wide open. She gestured at the nurse to leave her alone with the doctor. She was breathing slowly and deeply, with intense consciousness and a lust for life, as if she were drinking the last drops out of the goblet of time. Her nostrils quivered gently. Her face was enlightened, every wrinkle vanished from it, as usually only happens after death.

Even before she spoke, the doctor knew that her mind was healthy again. She stretched her transparent hand out towards him. 'I thank you for all of your care and sympathy, and for letting me be in peace. Here in your institution I was less insane than I have ever been in the whole of my life. I thought great things, saw wonderful things. Dreams and visions are life too, of course. Like Siegfried,[2] the language of the birds was bestowed upon me.'

She pointed to a book lying on her dresser. He brought it to her.

'After my husband's death, I started writing a diary. Please, burn it. You are a psychologist. If you'd like to know how and why my mind came to be so disturbed, then read it before you get rid of it. Nobody else should read it.'

He took the book out of her hand.

'I don't want to be buried', she said after a pause. 'Burnt. Blazing up in flames – in flames! That's what I want.'

And after another pause: 'Do many women die on the cross just to end up dead like the poor thief, or do they do it for others, like our Saviour?'

---

[2] Siegfried, the hero of the medieval epic *Nibelungenlied*, is known for his superhuman strength and his slaying of a dragon. Hedwig Dohm is most likely referencing the representation of the hero in Richard Wagner's opera, *Siegfried* (1876), where he acquires the ability to understand the language of birds after having bathed in the dragon's blood.

Ihre Augen blickten weit hinaus, groß und glänzend, und blieben am Firmament hängen, als ob sie von oben eine Antwort erwartete. Dann senkten sie sich langsam und nahmen den Ausdruck seherischer, in's Innerste schauender Verzücktheit an. "Ja – für die Andern – die andern Frauen."

Sie bewegte leise die Lippen. Der Arzt meinte, sie betete, und ging still hinaus.

Wissenschaftliche Neugierde und persönliches Interesse an der Sterbenden trieb ihn, das Tagebuch sofort zu lesen. Hier sein Inhalt.

* * *

Her eyes gazed off into the distance, big and bright, lingering on the Heavens, as if she were expecting an answer from up above. Then, as they slowly lowered, they took on the raptured expression of a seer, looking deep within. 'Yes – for the others – the other women.'

She moved her lips quietly. The doctor thought she was praying and silently left the room.

Driven by scientific curiosity and personal interest in the dying woman, he began reading the diary right away. This is what it said.

Ich muss schreiben – ja – ich muss! Sonst – – was sonst? Ich weiß es nicht. Bin ich herzkrank? Oder kommt es vom Hirn? Das innere Nagen, diese Empfindung des Verblutens, Erlöschens, und dann wieder die wirbelnde Unruhe. Krankheit ist es. Was für eine Krankheit?

Schreiben muss ich, ich kann ja mit Niemandem sprechen. Und könnte ich es, ich täte es nicht, nein, nie, um keinen Preis. Lachen würde man, lachen über die alte Frau, die froh sein sollte, dass sie das liebe Leben hat.

Ein alter Mann, das ist ein Mensch, der nicht mehr lange lebt, dessen Tage gezählt sind, aber er lebt! Eine alte Frau aber, die arm ist und Witwe, die ist so gut wie tot. Wozu lebt sie noch! Ob das an mir frisst, dass ich noch da bin, ohne zu wissen, wozu?

Ja, ich muss schreiben, damit ich nicht verrückt werde. Lebte ich dreihundert Jahre früher, ich würde denken, ich wäre besessen. Wovon? Von dem Teufel? Es ist doch nichts Böses in mir.

Ist es der Tod? Schüttelt mich der wilde Schauder der Natur vor dem Ende? Nein, ich fürchte das Ende nicht. Es ist nichts Grinsendes, Furchteinflößendes, das mich aufreibt. Etwas Starkes ist's, wundersam Drängendes, etwas, das an's Licht will. Geburtswehen? Was will geboren werden? Ich weiß es nicht.

Nur ruhig, ruhig! Ich schreibe ja, um ruhig zu werden.

Warum will ich eigentlich nicht verrückt werden? Gibt es nicht Wahnvorstellungen, berückende, schöne? Wenn ich mir nun einbildete, ich wäre – – Fort! Fort! Ich will sie ja loswerden, diese Verworrenheiten, die schwarzen Schatten und auch die leuchtenden Erscheinungen.

I must write – yes – I must! Otherwise – – otherwise what? I don't know. Am I heart-sick? Or does it come from the brain? The inner gnawing, this feeling of bleeding out, dying off, and then again, that whirling disquiet. It's illness. What kind of illness?

I must write, there's no way I can speak to anyone. And if I could, I wouldn't, no, never, not at any price. They'd laugh, laugh at the old woman who should count herself lucky to still be alive.

An old man, now that's a person who won't live much longer, whose days are numbered, yet he's alive! But an old woman who is poor and widowed? She's as good as dead. What does she live for! How it eats away at me to still be here without knowing – for what?

Yes, I have to write so I don't go mad. If I were living three hundred years ago, I would think I was possessed. But by what? the Devil? There isn't anything evil inside me.

Is it Death? Is it that wild shudder of Nature when faced with the end that's running through me? No, I don't fear the end. It's nothing sneering or terrifying that's chipping away at me. It's something stronger, something magnificently determined, something that wants to come to the light. Birthing pains? What is it that wants to be born? I don't know.

But peace! peace! I'm writing to find peace.

Why do I actually not want to go mad? Aren't there delusions that are enchanting, beautiful? If I just imagine that I'm – – Away! Away! I do want rid of them, these confusions, the black shadows along with the bright visions.

Kalt und nüchtern will ich prüfen, wie das kam, dass ich so geworden bin. Eine Art Nekrolog will ich von mir schreiben. Ich bin ja am Ende. Es kann nichts mehr kommen. Ich will einfach das Leben von Agnes Schmidt erzählen, die 54 Jahre alt ist und seit zwei Jahren Witwe mit einem Einkommen – Lebensversicherung und Pension eingerechnet – von 2500 Mark.

Erzählenswertes in meinem Leben! Gibt es das? Und was wäre das?

Ich habe lange dagesessen mit der Feder in der Hand und mich besonnen. Nichts, nichts!

Bin ich wirklich Agnes Schmidt? Ganz sicher Agnes Schmidt? Ich war es ganz bestimmt, bis mein Mann starb. Und nun, allmählich ist mir als schwände Agnes Schmidt immer mehr aus meinem Gesichtskreis, in weite Fernen hinaus, ein Schatten, der vor mir her ist, und der Schatten wird immer fahler, dünner, und an seine Stelle –

Ruhig! Ruhig! Ja, wie kam das! Es war doch von jeher Alles so in fester, schöner Ordnung gefügt. Ein so einfaches, gut und ganz ausgefülltes Leben, das meine.

Ich will mit dem Anfang anfangen, mit dem Kinde Agnes. Ein braves Kind, ein sanftes und ein hübsches Kind. Ich habe meinen Eltern keine Sorge gemacht. Ich tat, was man von mir verlangte. Sie zogen mir aber den Bruder vor, und wenn ich später weder Musik noch Zeichnen noch Sprachen oder sonst etwas lernte, so war es, weil dem Bruder Alles, was gespart werden konnte, zu gute kam. Jetzt weiß ich, warum man mir den Bruder vorzog; weil er der Sohn war und ich nur die Tochter. Und der Sohn machte den Eltern viel Kummer, den größten, als er starb, kaum zwanzigjährig. Ich glaube bestimmt, die Eltern hätten es weniger bitter empfunden, wenn ich gestorben wäre. Ich konnte doch nichts dafür. Seitdem wurde ich noch braver, ich hatte auch kaum Zeit und Gelegenheit, anders zu sein. Das Gehalt meines Vaters – er war Kanzleirat – war klein.

Cold and sober, I want to examine how I became like this. I want to write a kind of obituary for myself. After all, I am at the end. Nothing more will come of this. I only want to recount the life of Agnes Schmidt, who is 54 years old, and has been a widow for two years with an income – life insurance and pension inclusive – of 2500 Marks.

Something worth recounting in my life? Is there such a thing? And what would it be?

I have long been sat here with a pen in my hand trying to recollect it. Nothing, nothing!

Am I really Agnes Schmidt? absolutely positively Agnes Schmidt? I most definitely was up until my husband died. And now it is as though Agnes Schmidt is gradually disappearing, more and more, from my view, into the far distance, a shadow in front of me, and the shadow is growing ever sallower and thinner, and in its place –

Quiet! Quiet! Yes, how did that happen! Everything had always been so firmly and beautifully organised. Such a simple, good and full life was mine.

Let me start at the beginning, with the child Agnes. A good child, a gentle and beautiful child. I caused my parents no trouble. I did exactly what I was told. But they favoured my brother, and if later on I learnt neither music, drawing, nor languages, nor anything else, it was because everything that could be saved up went to my brother. Now I know why they preferred my brother: because he was the son, and I was just the daughter. And the son caused my parents a lot of grief, the greatest when he died, barely twenty years old. I know for certain that my parents would have felt less bitter if I had been the one who died. As if I could control that. After his death I became even more well-behaved, I had no time or opportunity to be any different. My father's salary – he was a law clerk – was small.

Die Mutter und ich, wir hielten getreulich Alles zusammen. Kaum zwölfjährig half ich schon in den Stunden, die mir die Schule freiließ, im Haushalt, in der Küche, bei der Wäsche. Ich tat auch Alles recht gern; es fiel mir gar nicht ein, dass es anders hätte sein können. Alle Mädchen, die wie wir in einfachen Verhältnissen lebten, taten so ziemlich dasselbe. Ich war heiter, zufrieden und kerngesund. Die Privatschule, in die man mich schickte, muss dürftig gewesen sein. Ich habe nie richtig orthographisch schreiben gelernt und auch sonst nichts Rechtes. Und doch verdankte ich dieser Schule hier und da eine Sonntagsstimmung, wenn wir die Klassiker lasen. Einmal musste ich ein Schiller'sches Gedicht deklamieren. Ich tat es mit glühenden Wangen und so pathetisch, dass die ganze Klasse lachte. Ich schämte mich, tat es nie wieder und leierte von da an die Gedichte herunter wie die Andern auch. Ich bin wohl immer scheu und empfindsam gewesen.

Ähnlich erregte es mich, wenn nachts der Mond auf mein Lager schien. Ich stand auf, stieg auf einen Tisch, der am Fenster stand, und sah herzklopfend hinaus in die silberne Traumwelt. Einmal fiel der Tisch um. Es gab großen Lärm im Hause. Ich wurde gestraft und erfuhr, dass ich etwas sehr Böses getan hatte. Und wenn der Mond mich wieder locken wollte, dann zog ich die Bettdecke über den Kopf. So lehrte man mich erkennen, was gut und böse ist.

Ich träumte oft, dass ich fliegen konnte, weit, weit fort, und so hoch, wie der Himmel ist. Ich ärgerte mich dann, wenn ich aufwachte. Es war so wunderschön gewesen, das Fliegen. Meine Mutter war gewiss eine brave Frau. Ich weiß nicht mehr viel von ihr. Doch erinnere ich mich, dass sie streng auf Ordnung und Schicklichkeit hielt. Was die Andern taten, das war für sie das Richtige. Es würde sie beunruhigt haben, wenn mein Kleid einige Zentimeter länger oder kürzer gewesen wäre als das der übrigen Schulkinder. Wir kleideten uns nach dem Kalender, nicht nach dem Thermometer. Die Mutter lebte eigentlich nur für den Vater. Der war wohl etwas verkümmert. Von mir nahm er kaum Notiz. Er wusste nicht, was er mit mir reden sollte. Ich glaube, er hielt nur Söhne für rechte Kinder.

My mother and I faithfully kept everything together. When I was barely twelve years old, I already helped in the hours I had free from school, in the household, in the kitchen, with the laundry. I did it gladly, it didn't occur to me it could have been any other way. All the girls who lived in humble circumstances like us did much the same. I was cheerful, happy, and in perfect health. The private school I was sent to must have been lacking. I never learnt how to write properly or anything else for that matter. And yet this school was to be thanked for my occasional cheerful mood when we read the Classics. One time I had to recite a poem by Schiller. I did it with glowing cheeks and such passion that the whole class laughed. I felt ashamed, never did it again, and from then on, I simply reeled off the poems like the others. I have always been shy and sensitive.

Similarly, it used to excite me when the moon shone on my bed at night. I would stand up, climb onto a table, which was by the window, and stare with my heart beating out into the silvery dream world. One time the table collapsed. There was a lot of noise in the house. I was punished and discovered that I had done something very bad. And when the moon tried to entice me again, I pulled the duvet over my head. That's how I was taught to recognize right from wrong.

I often dreamt that I could fly, far, far away, and as high as the sky. I would get upset when I woke up. It had been so wonderful to fly. My mother was certainly an upright woman. I don't remember much about her anymore. Yet I recall that she was strict about order and decorum. Whatever everyone else did was the right thing for her. It would have unsettled her if my dress had been a single centimetre longer or shorter than the other schoolchildren. We dressed according to the calendar, rather than the thermometer. The mother only really lived for the father's sake. He was probably somewhat stunted. I was hardly of notice to him. He did not know to say to me. I think he only viewed sons as proper children.

Mädchen müssen doch wohl untergeordnet sein, da Eltern immer enttäuscht sind, wenn ihnen Töchter anstatt Söhne geboren werden.

Ab und zu, an Sonntagnachmittagen durfte ich lesen. Als ich herangewachsen war, las ich unsinnig gern die Romane von der Marlitt. Marlitt'sche Romane und an Festtagen Apfelkuchen mit Schlagsahne, das waren die Extrafreuden der Tochter des Kanzleirats.

Als ich noch sehr jung war, bewarb sich ein junger Beamter, der im Bureau meines Vaters arbeitet, um mich. Meine Eltern meinten, er wäre tüchtig und rechtschaffen und den Ansprüchen, die ein einfaches, mittelloses Mädchen machen könne, angemessen.

Er gefiel mir, eine Verlobung gefiel mir noch mehr. Was mich aber unwiderstehlich lockte, war die Vorstellung von dem weißen Atlaskleid mit der Schleppe, von dem Myrtenkranz und dem Schleier.

Die Ehe lag noch in so weiter Ferne. Was sie sei, und was sie für Anforderungen an das Weib stelle, darnach fragte ich nicht, und Niemand belehrte mich darüber.

In gelassenem Frohsinn flossen die vier Jahre meines Brautstandes dahin. Während dieser Zeit war ich noch viel beschäftigter als früher. Ich nähte meine ganze Ausstattung selbst, wie es sich gehörte. Ich lernte kochen und schneidern, um für alle Fälle gerüstet zu sein, wie meine Mutter sagte. Und Abend für Abend kam mein Bräutigam, Eduard Schmidt, und ich schnitt und belegte ihm die Butterbrote, und er kam mir so recht gescheut vor, weil er soviel wusste, wovon ich keine Ahnung hatte.

Ich hatte Eduard wirklich lieb. Ich glaube, jeder Mensch muss irgend Jemand lieb haben; für mich war es Eduard.

Eines Tages aber war Hochzeit. Nach einer kurzen Hochzeitsreise bezogen wir eine kleine Parterrewohnung in der Philippstraße. Die Zimmer lagen nach Norden. Die Sonne schien nicht hinein.

Girls must be subordinate, it seems, as parents are always disappointed when daughters are born to them instead of sons.

Every now and then, on Sunday afternoons, I was allowed to read. When I was growing up, I particularly liked reading Marlitt's novels.[3] Marlitt's novels and apple pie with whipped cream on holidays: those were the simple pleasures of the clerk's daughter.

A young clerk who worked in my father's office asked for my hand, when I was still very young. My parents thought him good and honest, a suitable match for a plain, penniless girl.

I liked him; I liked the idea of an engagement even more. But what was most irresistible to me was the prospect of the white satin dress with train, of the myrtle wreath and veil.

Marriage was still a distant thought. What that was and what it demanded of a woman, I did not ask, nor did anybody enlighten me.

Those four years of engagement passed by in serene happiness. During that time, I was busier than ever before. I embroidered my entire trousseau by myself, as was proper. I learned to cook and make clothes, so that I was prepared for every eventuality, as my mother used to say. And night after night, my bridegroom, Eduard Schmidt, would visit us and I would set down his bread, all buttered and cut into pieces, and he would seem so clever to me, for he knew so much that I had no idea about.

I was really fond of Eduard. I believe that every person must be fond of someone; for me, that someone was Eduard.

But then the wedding day came. After a short honeymoon, we moved into a small, ground-floor apartment near the Tiergarten. The rooms were north facing. No sunshine got in.

---

[3] E. Marlitt, pseudonym of Friederieke Henriette Christiane Eugenie John (1825-1887), was a popular writer in nineteenth-century Germany. Her stories most often focus on a young woman, striving for freedom and education.

In der ersten Zeit unserer Ehe war ich weniger heiter und zufrieden als im Brautstand. Ich hatte auch Eduard weniger lieb. Ich bin wohl kalt und scheu von Natur, und mein innerstes Wesen sträubte sich gegen Vieles, was zur Ehe gehört. Als ich ihm zwei Kinder geboren, sah Eduard ein, dass für einen noch größeren Zuwachs der Familie sein Gehalt nicht ausreichen würde. Und von da an lebten wir friedlich und gut mit einander, in einer wolkenlosen Ehe, die dreiunddreißig Jahre währte.

Wenn ich jetzt an ihn zurückdenke, meine ich, dass er ein ehrenwerter Mann war, ganz Bureaukrat. Er hatte jederzeit die Ansichten, die ihm als Beamter zukamen, nicht aus Liebedienerei, sondern aus ehrlichem Pflichtgefühl. Er war meiner Mutter so wahlverwandt wie möglich. Dass er, von seiner Superiorität mir gegenüber überzeugt, etwas eigenwillig und streng in seiner Anforderung an mich war, tat dem Frieden unserer Ehe keinen Abbruch. Ich machte ihm nie Opposition, richtete vielmehr Alles ganz so ein, wie er es wünschte. Er hatte sich im Interesse der Seinigen hoch in der Lebensversicherung eingekauft. Da musste ich fleißig die Hände rühren, damit wir auskamen. Ich tat, was ich konnte, es war auch wirklich nicht zu viel. Alle jungen Frauen, die unbemittelte Beamte geheiratet hatten, taten dasselbe, und ich tat es gern. War ich doch von Jugend auf daran gewöhnt.

Gegen Abend war ich immer bereit, mit Eduard spazieren zu gehen. Nur ging er meistens so schnell, dass es mich etwas anstrengte. Vor dem Schlafengehen spielte er gern Karten. Ich spielte nicht gern Karten, freute mich aber, dass ich ihm den kleinen Dienst leisten konnte. Und dann war ich so müde und schlief so gut. Ich war gesund, mein Mann war glücklich und zufrieden, meine Töchter Grete und Magdalene gediehen. Herzige muntere Kinder, die ich von ganzem Herzen liebte, die aber dafür sorgten, dass ich tüchtig schaffen musste.

I was less cheerful and content as a new bride than I was as a fiancée. I was also less fond of Eduard. I am, perhaps, cold and timid by nature and my innermost essence struggled against much of what is expected in a marriage. After I bore him two children, Eduard realised that his salary would not be sufficient for an even larger family. And from that point on we lived peacefully and well with one another, in a cloudless marriage that lasted thirty-three years.

When I think back to him now, I believe he was a respectable man, a real bureaucrat. He always held views suitable for a civil servant, not out of servility, but out of a real sense of duty. He was as congenial as possible with my mother. That he, convinced as he was of his superiority to me, was somewhat wilful and strict in what he demanded of me, did not disturb the happiness of our marriage. I never opposed him, in fact I arranged things just as he wished. He had taken out a hefty life insurance policy for his family's sake. I then had to work very diligently so that we could get by. I did what I could, it was really not all that much. All the young women who married civil servants with humble means did much the same, and I was happy to. I was used to it from childhood.

In the evenings I was always prepared to go for a walk with Eduard. Only, he often walked so quickly that it was somewhat of a strain for me. He liked to play cards before going to bed. I did not like to play cards, but I was happy that I could perform this small service for him. And then I would be so tired and would sleep so well. I was healthy, my husband was happy and content, my daughters Grete and Magdalene were thriving. Darling, lively children, whom I loved with my whole heart, but who made sure I was always hard at work!

Und ein Tag war wie der andere. Wie auf Rollen glitt mein Leben dahin, schnell, schnell. Nur wenn ich ein paar Stunden hinter einander an der Nähmaschine sitzen musste, das machte mich nervös. Dann hatte ich zuweilen eine merkwürdige Empfindung: ein rieselndes Zittern in den Nerven. Der Faden riss, die Nadel fiel mir aus der Hand, und ich horchte auf, als müsste etwas geschehen, was, hätte ich nicht sagen können. Ein vages Erstaunen über die Frau, die da an der Nähmaschine saß und so emsig stichelte, ein plötzliches Michfremdfühlen in der lieben gewohnten Umgebung. Doch das ging immer schnell vorüber.

Ich entbehrte eigentlich nichts, als dass ich so wenig zum Lesen kam. Ich las so gern. Ich tröstete mich aber damit, dass, wenn meine Mädchen groß oder verheiratet wären, dann würde ich Zeit, soviel Zeit haben zum Lesen, ganze Nachmittage und Abende.

Und sie wurden groß, und ich konnte weniger als je lesen; denn nun gingen sie in Gesellschaften, und wir mussten die Einladungen erwidern. Das Herrichten der Toiletten, das Sorgen um die Mahlzeiten nahmen mich völlig in Anspruch. Das war auch die Zeit, wo mir oft das Herz schwer wurde, um meiner Mädchen willen. Das eine Mal ängstigte ich mich, Magdalene könne sich mit einem Ausländer, dessen Charakter keine Garantie für eine gute Ehe bot, verloben. Das andere Mal quälte mich die Vorstellung, dass der junge Fabrikherr, der Grete schon so lange den Hof machte und dem ihr Herz gehörte, vielleicht nur ein leichtfertiges Spiel mit ihr triebe. Drei Jahre dauerte dieses Bangen und Unbehagen, eine Zeit, in der ich ganz in den Leiden und Freuden meiner Töchter aufging. Schließlich wendete sich Alles zum Guten. Grete heiratete den jungen Fabrikherrn und Magdalene einen Amtsrichter. Betrübend war es für mich, dass keine von beiden in Berlin blieb.

Ich wunderte mich im Stillen etwas, dass sie gerade diesen Männern ihre Neigung geschenkt hatten, war aber doch froh, sie gut versorgt zu wissen.

And one day was like the next. My life glided along as if on wheels, fast, fast. It was only when I had to sit at the sewing machine for a few hours at a time that I felt nervous. Then I would sometimes have a strange sensation: a crawling tremor in my nerves. The thread broke, the needle fell out of my hand, and I listened as if something were about to happen, I just didn't know what. A vague astonishment at the woman sitting at the sewing machine and stitching so diligently, a sudden feeling of alienation from my familiar surroundings. But that always passed quickly.

I didn't really miss anything except that I didn't get to read so much. Oh how I used to love reading! But I consoled myself with the fact that when my girls were grown up or married, I would have so much time to read, whole afternoons and evenings.

And they did indeed grow up, and I could read less than ever, because now they were attending parties, and we also had to return the invitations. Taking care of their toilettes and of the meals took up all of my time. This was also the time when my heart was often heavy for the sake of my girls. One time I was afraid that Magdalena might get engaged to a foreigner, whose character was no guarantee of a good marriage. The other time I was tormented by the idea that the young factory owner, who had been courting Grete for a long time and to whom her heart belonged, might be playing a frivolous game with her. This anxiety and unease lasted three years, a time in which I was completely absorbed in the joys and sufferings of my daughters. In the end, everything turned out well. Grete married the young factory owner and Magdalena married a magistrate. It was unfortunate for me that neither of them stayed in Berlin.

Sometimes I wondered quietly why they had given their affections to these men in particular, but still, I was glad to know that they were well provided for.

Heiterer als je sah ich in die Zukunft. Grete und Magdalene wollten uns oft in Berlin besuchen, und ich wollte alljährlich einmal mit Eduard zu ihnen kommen.

Und wir würden reisen. Eduard versprach es mir. Bisher hatten wir nur ab und zu in der Nähe von Berlin auf vier Wochen eine Sommerfrische gehabt, in Misdroy oder im Harz, wohin wir regelmäßig das Dienstmädchen mitnahmen, um selbst zu wirtschaften. Das hatte in dem kleinen Badeorte manches Belästigende mit sich gebracht. Ich hatte immer doppelte Arbeit gehabt. Und wenn nachmittags Spaziergänge unternommen wurden, war ich schon müde und blieb am liebsten zu Haus. Und begleitete ich ab und zu die Meinigen, meine Gedanken blieben doch zurück, bei dem Dienstmädchen, bei dem Abendessen. Auch musste ich mich anstrengen, mit den Andern Schritt zu halten.

Nun sollte Alles anders werden. Wir hatten jetzt Geld genug. Weit, weit fort wollten wir reisen, in die Schweiz, nach Tirol, vielleicht bis nach Oberitalien.

Es sollte nicht sein. Wenige Wochen nach der Verheiratung der Töchter erkrankte Eduard. Er genas nicht mehr. Ein Rückenmarksleiden entwickelte sich, das ihn acht Jahre an's Krankenbett fesselte. Acht Jahre lang pflegte ich ihn. Mit dem liebevollen Eigensinn des Kranken nahm er von Niemand, außer mir, auch nur die kleinste Handreichung. Er aß nur, was ich ihm selbst bereitete, und war doch unzufrieden, wenn ich das Krankenzimmer verlassen musste. Armer, armer Eduard! Nie war jede Stunde meines Lebens so ausgefüllt, als während dieser langen Krankheit.

The future looked brighter than ever. Grete and Magdalene wanted to visit us in Berlin often, and I wanted to go to them once a year with Eduard.

And we would travel. Eduard had promised. Until then, we had only had the occasional, four-week summer holiday near Berlin, usually taking the maid with us so that we could cater for ourselves. That brought many a nuisance to the small bathing resort. I always had double the work. And so when the family would go for an afternoon walk, I was already tired, and preferred to stay in. And when I occasionally did accompany them, my thoughts still stayed back at the house, with the maid and the dinner. Also, it was difficult for me to keep up with the others.

Everything was meant to be different now. We had enough money. We wanted to travel far, far away, to Switzerland, Tirol, maybe even as far as northern Italy.

It was not to be. A few weeks after our daughters were both married, Eduard fell ill. He did not recover. He developed a pain in his spine which left him bedridden for eight years. For eight years, I looked after him. With the loving obstinacy of the sick he accepted from no one, except me, even the slightest assistance. He only ate what I had prepared for him myself yet was disgruntled whenever I had to leave the sickroom. Poor, poor Eduard! Never was each hour of my life so filled up as during this long period of sickness.

Von einer Reise zu meinen Töchtern konnte keine Rede sein. Ab und zu kamen sie wohl auf einen Tag nach Berlin. Es war aber Alles so traurig im Hause, und ich hatte so gar keinen Augenblick Zeit für sie, dass ich nicht wagte, ihnen zuzureden, länger zu bleiben oder häufiger zu kommen. Die Fabrik von Gretes Mann lag in der Nähe von Magdeburg, und Magdalenes Mann war Amtsrichter in einer kleinen hannoverschen Stadt.

Im Laufe der acht Jahre schenkten sie mir vier Enkel. Ich lernte sie nicht kennen.

Meine Schwiegersöhne sah ich nur ganz flüchtig, wenn sie in Begleitung ihrer Frauen dem armen Kranken einen kurzen Besuch abstatteten. Ich war so ungeschickt, verstand auch so gar nicht, mich herauszureißen und etwas zu ihrer Zerstreuung zu tun.

Eduard starb. Ich habe innig um ihn getrauert. Unfasslich war's mir in der ersten Zeit, dass er nicht mehr da war, ich ihn nicht mehr pflegen sollte. Bei Tage lief ich ruhelos durch die Zimmer, immer aufhorchend, ob er mich rufen würde. Oft, wenn ich Nachts erwachte, stürzte ich an sein Bett. Still, leer Alles um mich her.

Meine Töchter hatten mich vom Begräbnis aus gleich mit sich nehmen wollen. Ich hatte sie gebeten, erst einige Zeit vergehen zu lassen, bis ich gefasster geworden. Sie sahen es ein und ließen mich. Ich musste versprechen, so bald als möglich zu kommen.

Einige Wochen noch hatte ich mit dem Ordnen des Nachlasses zu tun, dann war ich fertig mit Allem. Ich war müde von dem schweren Tagewerk der letzten Jahre, ich durfte mich ausruhen. Warum kam die Ruhe nicht? Sie kam nicht. Und nun fing es an, ganz allmählich, das Seltsame, das Nagen, das Grübeln, das Schreckliche.

Travelling to visit my daughters was out of the question. Now and then, they would come to Berlin for a day. But everything in the house was so sad and I had so little time to spare for them, that I didn't dare suggest they stay longer or come more often. The factory in which Grete's husband worked was near Magdeburg and Magdalene's husband was a magistrate in a small town near Hannover.

In the space of eight years, they gifted me with four grandchildren. I never got to know them.

I only ever saw my sons-in-law fleetingly when they accompanied their wives on brief visits to see my poor, sick husband. I was so unused to company, I didn't even know how to pull myself away from my duties to entertain them.

Eduard died. I mourned him in my heart. At first, I couldn't grasp that he was no longer there, that I was no longer supposed to look after him. By day, I restlessly wandered through the rooms, always listening out to see if he would call for me. When I woke at night, I would often hurry to his bedside. Everything around me, silent, empty.

My daughters had wanted to take me with them straight after the funeral. I had asked them to give me some time until I became more composed. They understood, let me be. I had to promise I'd come as soon as possible.

It took me a few weeks to get the estate in order and then I was done with it all. I was weary from all the hard work of the last few years. I could let myself rest. Why did rest not come? It did not come. And then it began, the gnawing, the brooding, the strangeness, the awfulness.

Ich saß stundenlang und tat nichts und dämmerte so hin. Dann lief ich von der Wohnung auf die Straße in die Wohnung. Ich hatte solche Unlust, zu meinen Töchtern zu reisen. Und zu mir konnten sie nicht kommen. Grete erwartete ihr drittes Kind, Magdalene konnte im Haushalt nicht einen Tag entbehrt werden. Sie wussten ja auch, ich war wohl, mir ging nichts ab. Mir geht ja auch wirklich nichts ab. Oder – was denn?

Ich hatte meinen Töchtern geschrieben, ich würde im Frühjahr kommen, im Frühjahr aber schrieb ich, dass ich erst im Herbst reisen würde. Jederzeit wäre ich herzlich willkommen, haben sie geantwortet.

Es war Alles so gut in meinem Leben gewesen. Kein großer Kummer hatte mich heimgesucht. Selbst Eduards Krankheit war ein sanftes, allmähliches, fast schmerzloses Erlöschen gewesen. Er hatte sich zuletzt noch so gefreut, als er den Titel Geheimrat erhielt. Ihn zu pflegen hatte mir wohlgetan.

Nun konnte ich lesen, lesen, so viel ich wollte. Und ich lese, Romane wie ich sie früher liebte, in der Art der Marlitt. Sie gefallen mir nicht mehr, ich lese oft mechanisch, ohne zu wissen was. Es ist mir so gleichgültig, was darin steht, aber so gleichgültig.

Ich machte feine Stickereien für die Kleider meiner Enkelchen. Grete und Magdalene bedankten sich sehr schön dafür, ich las aber zwischen den Zeilen, dass diese Art der Stickerei nicht mehr Mode sei. Und ich sollte meine armen, alten Augen schonen, schrieben sie. Meine armen, alten Augen sind doch aber ganz gesund. Ich habe das Sticken aufgegeben.

I sat for hours on end, doing nothing, drifting off. Then I'd wander from the apartment to the street and back again, from the street to the apartment. I had not the slightest inclination to go and visit my daughters. And they couldn't come to me. Grete was expecting her third child, Magdalene's household couldn't do without her for even a day. And they knew I was fine on my own, I had everything I needed. And I did have everything I needed. Didn't I?

I had written to my daughters, saying I'd come in the spring but when spring came, I wrote that I wouldn't be travelling until autumn. I'd be welcome any time, they replied.

Everything about my life had been good. I hadn't been afflicted by any major sorrows. Even Eduard's illness had been a gentle, gradual, almost painless fading away. He had never been as pleased as when he received the title of Privy Councillor. It had done me a world of good looking after him.

I could read, read, as much as I wanted. And I do, novels like the ones I loved in the past, the same kind as Marlitt's. But I no longer enjoy them, I often read them mechanically without taking them in. I hardly care what they're about, hardly at all.

I embroidered my grandchildren's clothes with delicate designs. Grete and Magdalene would thank me warmly for them, but I could read between the lines that this kind of embroidery was no longer in fashion. I should protect my poor old eyes, they would write. But my poor old eyes are perfectly well. I gave up embroidery.

Was nun? Ich begieße die Blumen, die Wasser genug haben, ich wische Staub von den Möbeln, auf denen kein Staub mehr liegt. Ich bleibe oft mitten im Zimmer stehen und sehe mich um, was ich tun könne. Wie hässlich mein Zimmer ist! So viel gehäkelte Deckchen! Ich nehme die gehäkelten Decken ab und lege sie wieder hin. Ich bin täglich auf den Kirchhof gegangen und habe die welken Blätter von den Blumen auf Eduards Grab gepflückt. Als ich merkte, dass diese Kirchhofgänge nur Gewohnheiten waren, gab ich sie auf.

* * *

What now? I water the flowers that have enough water, I wipe dust from the furniture that has no more dust on it. I often stand in the middle of the room and look around to see what can be done. Oh, how ugly my room is! So many crocheted doilies! I pick the doilies up and then lay them back down again. I used to go to the church-yard daily and pick the withered leaves from the flowers on Eduard's grave. When I realised that these churchyard trips were only out of habit, I gave them up.

Gestern fiel mein Blick zufällig in den Spiegel. Ich erschrak. Mein Gott, ich war ja eine alte Frau. So viel Falten und Runzeln. Seit wann war ich's denn? Wie schnell das kommt. Ich hatte bisher nie an mein Äußeres gedacht. Und wie dürftig, geschmacklos mein Anzug war! Das schwarz wollene Kleid mit der langen Taille, den engen Ärmeln und der schwarz seidenen Schürze darüber, der kleine, altmodische weiße Kragen mit der großen Porzellanbrosche, auf der Gretes Bild gemalt war, aber ganz unähnlich. Und das schwarze Filetnetz über meinem glattgestrichenen, grauen Haar. Hässlich und alt! das war ich.

Ich stehe oft lange, lange am Fenster und sehe die Menschen vorübergehen. Sonderbar, Keiner weiß, dass ich hier oben stehe und ihm nachsehe. Und Keiner weiß vom Andern, Keiner von Keinem.

Wusste ich denn viel von Eduard? Was wusste ich denn? Dass er gern Rührei mit Schinken aß und dass ich ihm die Taschentücher immer nach der Nummer in den Schrank legen musste, sonst wurde er böse.

Und er – was wusste er von mir? Von mir war ja nichts zu wissen. Wir waren beide rechtschaffene Leute, die ihre Pflicht taten.

Und diese angstvolle Unruhe nun, als hätte ich ein böses Gewissen? Wem tat ich was zu Leide? Oder ist es doch, weil Eduard starb? Im Anfang ja, da überfiel mich oft die schaudernde Verwunderung darüber, dass er tot war. Nun aber sind mir fast seine Gesichtszüge entschwunden. Gewaltsam will ich meine Gedanken zu ihm hindrängen, sie finden nicht, woran sie sich klammern können. Ich will an Grete, an Magdalene denken. Aber es sind nur die Kinder und die jungen Mädchen, deren Bilder mir vorschweben. Ihr Frauenleben kenne ich ja nicht. Ich betrachte die Photographien meiner Enkel, die ich nie gesehen; die Vorstellung, dass es die Kinder meiner Töchter sind, vermag nichts über mich.

Ich suche nach Erinnerungen aus meiner Kindheit, aus meinem Eheleben – nichts. Ich lese Eduards Briefe – nichts. Die Briefe meiner Töchter – nichts! Nichts!

Yesterday my gaze happened to land on the mirror. I jumped. My God, I was really an old woman. So many lines and wrinkles. Since when was I like this? how quickly this comes on! Until now I had never thought about my appearance. And how paltry and tasteless my clothing was! The black woollen dress with the low waistline, the tight sleeves and the black silk apron on top, the small, white, old-fashioned collar with the large porcelain brooch, that had Grete's portrait painted on it – a very poor likeness. And the black net over my flattened grey hair. Ugly and old! that's what I was.

I often stand at the window for a long, long time and watch people go by. How odd that no one knows I am standing up here and watching them. And no one knows anything of the other, no one knows anything of anyone.

Did I know much of Eduard? What did I know? That he liked to eat scrambled eggs and ham, that I always had to put his handkerchiefs in a specific order in the wardrobe otherwise he would get cross.

And Eduard – what did he know of me? Well, there wasn't anything to know of me. We were both respectable people who did our duty.

And why now this fearful disquiet, as though I have a guilty conscience? To whom did I ever cause harm? Or rather is it because Eduard died? At first, I was overcome with shuddering astonishment at the fact he was dead. But now his features have almost vanished from my mind. I want to forcefully shove my thoughts towards him; they don't find anything they can cling onto. I want to think about Grete, about Magdalene. But it is only the children and the young girls whose images float before me. I'm just not acquainted with their lives as women. I examine the photographs of my grandchildren, whom I never saw; the idea that they are the children of my daughters has no effect on me.

I search for memories from my childhood, from my married life – nothing. I read Eduard's letters – nothing. The letters from my daughters – nothing! nothing!

Aber etwas muss doch sein, irgend etwas.

Ich gebe es auf, mich zu beschäftigen. Ich nähe nicht mehr. Ich esse, was das Mädchen mir gerade vorsetzt. Ich begieße die Blumen nicht mehr. Sie vertrocknen. Immerzu. Ich vertrockne ja auch. Wenn Bekannte von früher mich besuchen, und sie sprechen von Wirtschaftsdingen, so wird es mir schwer, ihnen zuzuhören, und ich begreife nicht, dass früher meine Gedanken an dem Wenden alter Stoffe und an der Ausnutzung von Fleischresten hingen. Wenn sie wiederkommen, die Bekannten, lasse ich mich vor ihnen verleugnen. Ich will allein sein.

Es ist etwas in mir wie ein vages Erinnern an Weitentlegenes, das vor langer, langer Zeit gewesen, vielleicht nur Träume, die ich einst geträumt und vergessen habe.

Mignon, die hatte Italien nie gesehen und sehnte sich dahin mit allen Fibern ihres Herzens. Das Heimatsgefühl lag ihr im Blut. Bin ich auch so eine alte Mignon, die – – Ja, ich suche, wo ich daheim bin. Komische Vorstellung: eine alte Mignon mit einer großen Porzellanbrosche und – –

Ich habe gefunden, wo ich daheim bin, daheim sein muss – bei meinen Kindern. Dahin gehöre ich. Ich schreibe nicht mehr. Ich will meine Enkel kennen lernen. Magdalene war immer so herzig und sinnig. Zu ihr kann ich vielleicht von meinen zerrütteten Nerven sprechen. Sie weiß wohl Rat. Morgen schon reise ich. Ich *freue* mich darauf, sehr freue ich mich.

* * *

But there just has to be something, anything.

I gave up keeping myself busy. I don't sew anymore. I eat whatever the maid puts in front of me. I don't water the flowers anymore. They're withering. Relentlessly. I'm withering just the same. Whenever acquaintances from before come to visit me, and they speak of household matters, it gets difficult for me to listen to them, and I cannot fathom that, before, my thoughts used to be filled with reusing old fabric and using up leftover meat. When they come back, these acquaintances, I will have them turned away. I want to be alone.

There is something in me like a vague recollection of distant things that were long, long ago, perhaps only dreams that I once dreamt and forgot.

Mignon had never seen Italy and longed for it with all the fibres of her heart.[4] The feeling of being home was in her blood. Am I such an old Mignon too, who – Yes, I'm looking for a home. Strange idea: old Mignon with a large porcelain brooch and – –

I have found where I belong, where I must belong – with my children. That's where I belong. I no longer write. I want to get to know my grandchildren. Magdalene was always so sweet and sensible. Perhaps I can talk to her about my shattered nerves. She probably knows what to do. I'm travelling tomorrow. I'm looking forward to it, I'm *really* looking forward to it.

* * *

---

[4] Mignon is a female character in Johann Wolfgang von Goethe's *Wilhelm Meisters Lehrjahre* (1795-1796) and, to this day, is considered as the archetypical romantic heroine.

Acht Wochen *später.*

Ich schreibe doch wieder. Es ist nur schlimmer geworden. Vier Wochen war ich bei Grete, und nun bin ich schon einen ganzen Monat bei Magdalene. Ich kenne jetzt die Art des Wahnsinns, zu der ich Anlage habe: Verfolgungswahn. Meine Töchter, meine Schwiegersöhne, meine Enkel, liebe, treffliche, frohe und glückliche Menschen alle, und doch – doch – ich möchte, ich wäre erst wieder fort, zu Hause. Es ist Alles so handfest bei ihnen, so nüchtern taghell.

Es machte mich gleich im Anfang nervös, dass meine lieben Kinder mich noch immer "Mämmchen" nennen. "Mutter," ein schönes Wort; "Mämmchen" ist, als nähme man die Mutter nicht ernsthaft, nur so wie eine drollige Alte, als verpflichte es zu nichts. Und Eugen und Heinrich, meine Schwiegersöhne, sagen Mamachen zu mir. Große, erwachsene, fremde Männer nennen mich Mama. Es ist wohl Sitte so. Grete und Magdalene, waren das wirklich noch ganz meine Töchter? Sie gehen allerwege in die Fußstapfen ihrer Männer. Sie sprechen mit ihren Worten, sie hören mit ihren Ohren, sie haben ihre Ansichten und Gewohnheiten angenommen.

Es ist gut, sehr gut, dass das so ist. Aber sie sind doch nun ganz neue Menschen geworden, und ich bin fast befangen ihnen gegenüber. Mein schlankes Lenchen ist jetzt stark, Grete aber hat sich zu einem echten, rechten Weltkind entwickelt, und so klug ist sie. Ich staune ihre Klugheit an. Sie schüchtert mich etwas ein, und Heinrich, ihr Mann, der schüchtert mich auch ein. Und er hat doch so viel Wohlwollen für mich, immer ist er um meine Gesundheit besorgt. Wenn er mit Grete einen Spaziergang oder einen Besuch machte, so meinte er, das sei nichts für Mamachen, Mamachen bleibe gewiss lieber bei den Enkeln. Er erlaubte auch nicht, dass ich mich der Abendluft aussetzte. Und da sie meist im Freien aßen, zog ich es dann vor, eine Stunde früher mit den Kindern zu Abend zu essen. Er will immer nicht glauben, dass ich noch ganz kräftig und gesund bin.

Eight weeks later.

I'm writing again after all. It's only gotten worse. I visited Grete for four weeks, and now I've been with Magdalene for a whole month. I now know the kind of madness I'm prone to: paranoia. My daughters, my sons-in-law, my grandchildren, dear, excellent, cheerful, and happy people, and yet – yet – I wish I were away again, at home. Everything is so tangible with them, so practical and bright as day.

It made me nervous right from the start that my dear children still call me 'Mämmchen.' 'Mutter' is a nice word, 'Mämmchen,' is as if you don't take your mother seriously, just like a droll old lady, as if it doesn't commit you to anything. And Eugen and Heinrich, my sons-in-law, call me 'Mamachen.' Big, grown-up, strange men call me 'Mama.' I guess it's the custom. Grete and Magdalene, were they really still my daughters? They always follow in the footsteps of their husbands. They speak with their words, they listen with their ears, they have adopted their views and habits.

It is good, very good, that it is this way. But they have now become completely new people, and I am almost self-conscious around them. My slender Lenchen is strong now, but Grete has developed into a real, true child of the world, and she is so clever. I marvel at her intelligence. She intimidates me a little, and Heinrich, her husband, intimidates me too. And yet he has so much goodwill for me, he's always worried about my health. When he went for a walk or a visit with Grete, he said it was nothing for Mamachen, Mamachen would certainly prefer to stay with her grandchildren. He also didn't allow me to expose myself to the evening air. And as they usually ate outside, I chose to have dinner with the children an hour earlier. He still doesn't want to believe that I'm still strong and healthy.

Ich merkte, Grete war es oft peinlich, wenn ich mich so viel in den Hinterzimmern aufhielt. Ich beruhigte sie darüber, ich wäre am liebsten bei den Kindern. Es war nicht ganz so. Ich bin nur lieber bei den Kindern als – – Ich kann trotz aller Gegenversicherungen das Gefühl nicht los werden, dass ich meine Schwiegersöhne ein wenig in ihrer häuslichen Intimität beeinträchtige, vielleicht nur deshalb, weil ich ihre Schwiegermutter bin und auch alt und eine arme Beamtenwitwe.

Anfangs kam ich abends öfter in Gretes Wohnzimmer und las da die Zeitung. Das Papier knitterte etwas. Ich sah, es machte Heinrich nervös.

Könnte ich ihnen nur wenigstens etwas leisten!

Meinem Lenchen, die in einfachen Verhältnissen lebt, wäre es gewiss angenehm, wenn ich die Kinder etwas beaufsichtigte oder das Einkochen der Früchte, das ich früher so gut verstand. Ach, ich bin so unlustig geworden zu Allem und auch gleich müde. Als ich neulich zu einem Kindergeburtstag einen Kuchen backen wollte, da missriet er, und die Kinder fielen mit Neckereien über mich her. Sie tanzten wie kleine Wilde um mich her und sangen den Gassenhauer: "Wir brauchen keine Schwiegermama." Und Alle lachten, die Erwachsenen auch, und es war auch wirklich so sehr drollig und doch – doch – Ich heiße hier immer nur die Schwiegermutter, und ich bin doch als Mutter da.

Ist es nicht auch drollig, wenn die Kleinen mich bei der Mutter anklagen: das Großmämmchen hat sich Cakes genommen, oder das Großmämmchen hat sich in Deinem Spiegel gesehen, Muttchen. Und Walterchen will nicht, dass ich bei Tisch Erdbeeren bekomme, weil dann für sein Kinderfräulein keine übrig bleiben.

I noticed that Grete often felt embarrassed by my spending so much time in the back rooms. I assured her that I liked being with the children best. This wasn't completely true. I only prefer being with the children to – – I can't shake the feeling that, despite all assurances on the contrary, I am encroaching somewhat on the domestic intimacy of my sons-in-law, perhaps simply because I am their mother-in-law, and also the poor, old widow of a civil servant.

I used to come into Grete's living room more often and read the newspaper there in the evenings. The paper would crinkle somewhat. I saw that it made Heinrich nervous.

If only I could at least be of some use to them!

My little Lene, who lives in humbler circumstances, would certainly be grateful if I supervised the children for a while, or the making of fruit preserves, which I had previously been so skilled at. I've lost my enthusiasm for everything now, and tire so quickly. Recently, when I wanted to bake a cake for one of the children's birthdays, it went wrong, and the children teased me mercilessly. They danced like little wild-things and sang the old tune: 'We don't need no mother-in-law.' And everyone laughed, the adults too, and it was really so very jolly and yet – yet – I was still nothing but a mother-in-law, and I had come here as a mother.

Isn't it also funny when the little ones tell on me to their mother: Großmämmchen helped herself to cake, or Großmämmchen looked at herself in your mirror, mummy. And little Walter doesn't want me to get strawberries at the dinner table, because then there won't be any left for his nanny.

Wie sich Alle immer darüber amüsieren. Ich nicht. Stumpf bin ich geworden, stumpf. Ich habe nicht einmal mehr Sinn für die naiven Schelmereien der Kleinen. Ich hatte mir eine Großmutter anders gedacht, die Kinder wahrscheinlich auch. Sie mögen mich nicht besonders gern. Das ist ganz natürlich. Ich bin nicht lustig, bringe ihnen nichts mit und weiß keine Märchen. Bloß weil ich ihre Großmutter bin und alt, das ist doch kein Grund, mich lieb zu haben. Sie spielen oft Krieg. Ich muss zuweilen den Feind vorstellen, den sie niederstechen. Und sie stechen und hauen mit ihren hölzernen Spießchen so tapfer auf mich ein, dass es mir ernstlich weh tut, ich lache aber und tue, als fände ich es reizend, sonst mögen sie mich noch weniger leiden, die herzigen Tollköpfe. Als ich neulich Walterchen etwas verbot, sagte er: "Dir gehorche ich nicht, Du bist ja nur eine Witwe!" Weises Kind. Eine Witwe, das heißt: Dein Mann ist tot. Du bist mit ihm begraben. Die indische Witwenverbrennung hat doch einen tiefen Sinn – noch heut, und nicht nur in Indien.

Ich bin keine Persönlichkeit. Ich bin Niemand, darum kann mich auch Niemand lieb haben, und auch meine Kinder – kaum – kaum.

Ab und zu habe ich Grete einen Rat in Bezug auf häusliche Einrichtungen geben wollen. Sie meinte aber, das sei zu meiner Zeit so gewesen, jetzt sei Alles rationeller geworden. Oder sie antwortete gar nicht, nickte mir nur freundlich zu und dachte wohl: wozu dem alten Mämmchen erst lange widersprechen. Und Magdalene, die hat immer dieselbe Einwendung: "Aber Eugen sagt –" Und Eugen sagt wirklich – St! Schwiegermutter!

How everyone amuses themselves over that. Not me. I have become dull – dull. I have no sense for the little ones or their silly games anymore. I had imagined a grandmother differently; the children probably had too. They don't especially like me. Which is unsurprising. I am not funny, did not bring them anything, and don't know any fairytales. Simply being their grandmother and an old woman is not reason enough for them to love me. They often play at war. Sometimes, I have to play the enemy which they stab down. And they stab me and hit me with their little wooden spears with such enthusiasm that it actually hurts, but I laugh about it and pretend to find it endearing; otherwise, they'll like me even less, the lovely little madcaps. When I tried to stop Walter from doing something recently, he said, 'I won't obey you, you're just some widow!' Wise child. A widow: that means, your husband is dead. You are buried with him. The burning of widows has a deep significance after all – still today, and not only in India.

I am not a person. I am no one, so no one can love me, not even my children – barely – barely.

Every now and then, I tried offering Grete advice about running the household. But she would say that was the way it was in my day, now everything has become more efficient. Or she wouldn't reply at all, just nodding sympathetically, probably thinking: why keep on contradicting old Mämmchen. As for Magdalene, she always had the same objection: 'But Eugen says –' What Eugen really says was – Tsk! Mother-in-law!

Einmal hatte ich bei Grete über ein Naturheilverfahren bei Kinder-krankheiten gesprochen. Da stand Heinrich auf und sagte: "Bitte, Mama, nur nichts Medizinisches." Und am Tage darauf redeten wir von Mädchen-Erziehung. Da stand er auch auf und sagte: "Nur nichts über Erziehung, dann noch lieber Medizinisches." Ich weiß nicht mehr, was ich reden soll, und werde still und einsilbig; nur so das Allereinfachste sage ich, über das Wetter, über das blühende Aus-sehen der Kinder, und ich sage das nur so mechanisch, damit man mich nicht für mürrisch und unzufrieden halten soll.

Ich ertappe mich zuweilen, dass ich laut mit mir selber spreche. Tun das vielleicht alte Leute so häufig, weil Andere sie nicht hören mö-gen?

Ein ander Mal, als bei Grete Gesellschaft war, hatte ich mir ganz feine, neue Handschuhe angezogen, um ihr Ehre zu machen. "Tu mir den Gefallen, Mamachen," sagte Heinrich, "und ziehe die Hand-schuhe aus, man sieht dann gleich, dass Du zur Familie gehörst." Ei-nen Augenblick fuhr es mir durch den Sinn: hat er den Hinterge-danken, dass ich in meiner dürftigen Erscheinung, als gebetener Gast, kompromittierend bin? Für eine Mutter oder Schwiegermutter ist man nicht verantwortlich. Die muss man hinnehmen, wie Gott sie gibt. Ich bereute gleich diesen Gedanken.

Er lobte seinen Gästen gegenüber laut meine Herzensgüte, wie ich acht Jahre so treu meinen Gatten gepflegt u.s.w. Das war mir ent-setzlich peinlich und verletzte mich wirklich. Und wieder dachte ich: Lobt er Dich etwa, wie eine Art Entschuldigung für Deine sonstige Kümmerlichkeit. Ich sage es ja – Verfolgungswahn!

Once, I'd been speaking to Grete about a natural remedy to help with childhood illnesses. Heinrich got up, saying 'Please, Mama, let's not start on anything medical.' The next day, we were talking about girls' education. He got up again, saying 'Nothing about education please, I'd rather we talk medicine.' I no longer know what I'm supposed to talk about and have become silent and monosyllabic; I only say the simplest of things, about the weather, about how grown up the children look, and I just say it mechanically so that no one can call me sullen or discontent.

Sometimes I catch myself talking to myself out loud. Perhaps elderly people often do that because no one else will listen to them?

Another time when there were guests at Grete's house, I had put on some very fine new gloves for her sake. 'Mamachen,' said Heinrich. 'Do me a favour and take off your gloves, will you? Then you'll look like you actually belong in the family.' For a moment the thought flashed through my mind: did he really mean to say that I, as an invited guest, was embarrassing him with my meagre appearance? No one is responsible for a mother or a mother-in-law. She must be accepted as God has given her. I immediately regret those thoughts.

He praised my goodness of heart in front of his guests, the way I so faithfully cared for my husband for eight years and so on and so forth. This was unspeakably humiliating for me and hurt me deeply. And once again, I thought: he's only praising you as a kind of apology for your otherwise pitiful existence. I'll say it again – paranoia!

Wenn ich von einem Spaziergang heimkomme und ein besonders feiner Besuch ist bei meinen Kindern, so gehe ich die Hintertreppe herauf, leise, damit mich Niemand hört. Es ist unbequem für sie, das alte Mämmchen dem Gast erst vorstellen zu müssen, und darnach weiß man nicht, was man mit ihr anfangen soll. Es bedrückt mich, dass ich so unbeholfen bin, so würdelos im grauen Haar. Die Paar Höflichkeitsphrasen, die ab und zu ein Besuchender an mich richtet, irritieren mich. Sie brauchen ja nicht mit mir zu reden. Sie sollen es nicht.

So herzlich war mein Gretel beim Abschied und Heinrich so wohlwollend freundlich, wenn auch etwas zerstreut. Die Kinder bliesen eine Fanfare – allerliebster Einfall – oder – Humor, altes *Mämmchen!* Humor!

Magdalene macht soviel Umstände mit mir. Sie hat sich um meinetwillen ihres Teppichs beraubt. Neulich klagte sie über kalte Füße. "Wozu hast Du denn Deinen Teppich?" fragte Eugen. Sie gab ihm einen Wink. Und dann merkte ich, dass sie Mittags nicht wie sonst ihr Glas Wein trank. Sie spart es sich am Munde ab, um es mir zu geben. Es entfuhr ihr neulich, so unwillkürlich.

Magdalene ist, wie ich war. Ich sehe mich bei ihr wie in einem Spiegel. Sie nimmt auch oft von einer Speise nichts, damit ihr Mann recht viel davon haben soll. Nur verfährt sie bei Allem praktischer. Sie weiß es so einzurichten, dass ihr Mann dahinter kommt, wenn sie ihm ein Opfer bringt. Ich war immer in Angst, er könne es merken. Und Alles tut sie rascher, munterer und bewusster, als ich es tat. Und ihr Mann – den liebt sie ganz anders, als ich Eduard liebte, ganz anders.

If I'm coming back from a walk and a particularly genteel visitor is there, I go up the backstairs, quietly, so that no one will hear me. It's awkward for them to have to introduce the old Mämmchen to their guest, and once they do, no one knows what's to be done with her. It pains me to be so gauche, so undignified, shrouded in grey hair. The handful of courteous platitudes that a visitor will sometimes throw my way irritate me. They don't actually need to speak to me. So, they shouldn't.

How affectionate my Gretel was at our goodbye, and Heinrich so benevolently friendly, though somewhat absent-minded. The children erupted into a fanfare – the sweetest idea – or – have a sense of humour, old *Mämmchen* – humour!

Magdalene makes such a fuss over me. She has rid herself of her rug for my sake. Recently she complained of having cold feet. 'Well, what have you done with your rug?' asked Eugen. She gave him a wink. And then I noticed that she wasn't drinking her glass of wine at midday like usual. She was saving it to give it to me. She's been making a habit of this recently, quite involuntarily.

Magdalene is just as I used to be. I see myself in her as in a mirror. She often takes nothing from a dish so that her husband can have plenty of it. But she is more practical in every matter. She knows how to arrange things so that her husband finds out when she makes a sacrifice. I was always afraid he might find out. And she does everything more quickly, more cheerfully and more consciously than I did. And her husband - she loves him quite differently from the way I loved Eduard, quite differently.

Er ist lustig, der Eugen, recht zu Scherzen aufgelegt. Meine beiden Schwiegersöhne, unerschöpflich sind sie in Schwiegermutter-Anekdoten. Eugen wundert sich immer so in seiner spaßhaften Art über meinen Appetit. Was Mamachen essen kann! Beneidenswert! Heinrich wunderte sich übrigens auch darüber. Er hielt lebhaften Appetit geradezu für eine Schwiegermuttereigenschaft.

Es scheint wirklich, dass ich unnatürlich viel esse. Es war mir peinlich. Ich gab mir eine Zeit lang Mühe, wenig zu essen, das gilt ja auch für zuträglicher. Neulich musste ich aber doch wohl zu wenig gegessen haben, vielleicht hatte es auch irgend einen anderen Grund, ich fühlte mich sterbensschwach und hatte eine Ohnmachtsanwandlung. Ich bat Magdalene um ein Glas Rotwein und, wenn es keine Umstände mache, um ein wenig Fleisch. Wie Eugen sich darüber amüsierte. Er kam gar nicht aus dem Lachen heraus. Eine Krankheit, die mit Rotwein und Beefsteak geheilt würde, solch eine Krankheit wünsche er sich auch. Und er erzählte es Jedem, der kam, und erregte viel Heiterkeit damit.

Sie leben in einfachen Verhältnissen, haben aber keine Sorgen, und doch sagte Eugen neulich: "Mamachen hat es gut, die kann so aus dem Vollen wirtschaften." Er findet es unrecht, dass ich so allein in Berlin hause, sie hätten doch das hübsche Fremdenzimmer. Es wäre auch nicht verständig, wenn eine einzelne alte Dame für sich allein fast 3000 Mark ausgäbe. Wozu z.B. die große Wohnung von drei Zimmern u.s.w.

Magdalene wies ihn zurecht. Ich hätte doch das Geld, um es mir für meine alten Tage angenehm und bequem zu machen.

He's funny, Eugen, quite disposed to making jokes. Both Heinrich and Eugen, their mother-in-law anecdotes are inexhaustible. Eugen is always amazed at my appetite in his humorous way. Oh, how Mamachen can eat! Enviable! Heinrich was also surprised at this, by the way. He thought a lively appetite was a defining characteristic of a mother-in-law.

It really seems that I eat unnaturally much. I was embarrassed. For a while I made an effort to eat little, which is considered healthier. Recently, however, I must have eaten *too* little, or perhaps there was some other reason why I felt deathly weak and had a fainting spell. I asked Magdalene for a glass of red wine and, if it would be no trouble, for a little meat. How it amused Eugen! He couldn't stop laughing. A disease that could be cured with red wine and beefsteak, he longed for such a disease! And he told everyone who visited and got a lot of laughter from it.

They live in humble circumstances, but are comfortable enough, and yet Eugen said the other day, 'Mamachen has it good, she can spend as she pleases.' He thinks it is unfair that I have a house in Berlin all to myself when they have such a nice guest room. Nor is it prudent for a single old lady to spend almost 3000 Marks on herself alone. Why the large three-bed apartment etc.?

Magdalene scolded him. I had the money, after all, so that I could live comfortably and conveniently in my old age.

Natürlich, er wolle ja *auch*, dass Mamachen es auf's Beste habe, und er mache wahrhaftig keinen Anspruch auf Lenes Anteil an der Lebensversicherungsrente. Wenn er mir aber jährlich 1500 Mark zurücklegte – er hätte Gelegenheit das Geld gut anzulegen – so könnte ich mir für das Ersparte ein Extravergnügen antun, reisen oder Ähnliches. "Und dann kannst Du mir auch ein Wiegenpferd kaufen," rief das Walterchen dazwischen, "so groß, wie's gar kein's gibt." Ich sollte mir die Sache überlegen, meinte Eugen, mein Ausbedingestübchen sei immer bereit.

Es war wirklich nur ein Stübchen, ein ganz kleines. Ich hatte ein Gefühl der Angst, er könne ein positives Versprechen von mir verlangen, und das wollte ich nicht geben.

Als ich neulich Abend meine Freude über den Duft der Lindenblüten äußerte, sagte er: "Fasse Dich nur, Mamachen," und er sagte es so komisch, dass wieder Alle lachten.

Neulich waren wir ausgefahren, die Pferde scheuten und bäumten sich hoch auf. Ich gebärdete mich ängstlich. "Gottes Wille geschehe," sagte Eugen lachend, um mir die Angst wegzuscherzen, "wenn Dir etwas Menschliches zustoßen sollte Mamachen, Deine Töchter sind ja versorgt, Du hast zwei reizende Schwiegersöhne" u.s.w.

Solche Scherze machen mich immer traurig.

Am traurigsten war ich vor einigen Tagen, als ich von einem plötzlichen, heftigen Übelsein befallen wurde und Magdalene den Arzt holen ließ. Eugen hörte so merkwürdig gespannt auf den Ausspruch des Arztes. Warum denn? Zu leben, wenn Einer wünscht, dass man tot wäre – schrecklich! Schrecklich! Aber er wünscht es ja gar nicht. Ich bin nur – ich habe nur –

Of course, *he* wanted Mamachen to have it best too, and he truly didn't want to make any claim on Lene's portion of the life insurance payments. But if he put aside 1500 Marks for me annually – he had the opportunity to invest the money well – then I could use the savings for some special treat, travelling or something like that. 'And then you can buy me a rocking-horse, too,' little Walter interrupted, 'bigger than any other!' I ought to think about it, Eugen said, my little room at their house was always ready.

It was really only a little room, a very small one. I felt anxious that he could demand a definitive promise from me, and I didn't want to make one.

The other evening, when I expressed my delight over the smell of the lime-blossoms, he said, 'Get a hold of yourself, Mamachen!', and he said it in such a funny way that everyone laughed again.

The other day, we were out in the cart, the horses shied away and reared up high. I grew afraid. 'God's Will be done,' laughed Eugen. Then to dispel my fear, he joked, 'Should anything happen to you, Mamachen, your daughters are well provided for, you have two charming sons-in-law,' and so on.

These kinds of jokes always make me sad.

I was at my saddest a few days ago, when I was struck down suddenly by a violent bout of sickness and Magdalene sent for the doctor. Eugen was strangely fascinated when listening to the doctor's orders. But why? To live when it is wished you were dead – terrible! Terrible! But he surely doesn't want that. I only am – I only have –

Neulich hörte ich durch die offene Tür, wie ein Herr zu meinem Schwiegersohn sagte: "Wie? Lebt die Mama Schmidt noch? Ich habe doch nie von ihr sprechen hören." Was hätten sie auch von mir sprechen sollen!

Humor, Mämmchen! Humor!

Ich bin böse auf mich, dass Eugens Scherze mich erregen. Ich war doch früher sanft und anspruchslos. Verliert man diese Eigenschaft im Alter?

Trefflich sind meine Schwiegersöhne, und ich bin ihnen innig dankbar, dass sie meine Töchter so glücklich machen. Aber fort muss ich, ja, ich muss! Ich bin nicht mehr unruhig, aber ich werde täglich stumpfer. Wie Einem Hände oder Füße einschlafen, so schläft etwas Geistiges in mir ein. Alles Blut aus dem Gehirn entweicht. Ich muss es bewegen, bewegen! In's Freie! In's Freie!

Vielleicht sind doch Kinder nur eine Episode im Leben einer Frau, und sie hören auf, Töchter zu sein, wenn sie Mütter geworden sind. Es ist fast ein Anachronismus, dass sie noch eine Mutter haben. Sie leben auch in einer andern Zeit, in einem andern Kreis. Darum ist die Mutter bei ihren Kindern nicht am Platz.

Nein, von meiner Nerven-Überreiztheit hätte ich eher zu jedem Fremden als zu meinen Kindern sprechen können. Sie würden gleich denken, ich wäre auf dem Wege, den Verstand zu verlieren. Hätten sie ganz Unrecht?

Morgen reise ich ab. Ich freue – – was wollte ich denn da schreiben? ach Gott!

* * *

The other day, through the open door, I heard a man speaking to my son-in-law: 'What? Is Mama Schmidt still alive? I've never heard anyone talk about her.' What should have been said about me!

Humour, Mämmchen! Humour!

I'm cross with myself for letting Eugen's jokes affect me. I used to be so gentle and unassuming. Is that quality lost as we grow old?

My sons-in-law are excellent, and, in my heart, I am grateful to them for making my daughters so happy. But I must go, yes, I must! I am no longer restless, but I grow duller with each day. Just like hands or feet fall asleep, something spiritual in me is falling asleep too. All the blood is leaking out of my brain. I must move it, move! Out into the open, be free!

But perhaps children are only one episode in a woman's life, and they stop being daughters once they have become mothers. It's almost anachronistic that they still have a mother. They live in a different time, move in a different circle. The mother is therefore out of place with her children.

No, on the topic of my overwrought nerves I would rather have spoken to any stranger than to my own children. They would both have thought I was losing my mind. Would they be entirely wrong?

I'm leaving tomorrow. I'm looking forward – – what did I want to write there? Oh God.

Wieder daheim. Nun wird's besser werden, viel besser. Ich bin nicht mehr wie eingeschlafen. Ich bin wach, beinah unternehmungslustig. Ich gehe viel aus, ich gehe in Galerien, in's Theater. Ich lese, ja, hauptsächlich lese ich. Ich hatte in der Zeitung Bücher erwähnt gefunden, russische, französische, skandinavische, die einen geistigen und sittlichen Umschwung bedeuten und das Leben schildern sollten, wie es wirklich ist. Wie es wirklich ist? Wäre das der Mühe des Schilderns wert? Ich habe in diesen Büchern gelesen, tagelang. Stellenweise fesselten sie mich bis zu krankhafter Aufregung, bis zu schaudernder Ergriffenheit. Dann wieder verstand ich nicht mehr. Wollte ich einen Gedankengang festhalten, er zerfloss wieder. Ich nahm mir auch nicht die Zeit, Seite für Seite aufmerksam zu lesen, ich blätterte nur in den Büchern. Ich habe ja keine Zeit. Ich will den Geist des Ganzen fassen, im Fluge. Ich bin wie gehetzt von Etwas, das immer hinter mir her ist – was? Tod, Geistesverwirrung, oder was sonst?

Eine Völkerwanderung von Ideen, Stimmungen, Gedanken stürzt über mich her. Wie? Diese Schriftsteller verwerfen, was bisher für unumstößlich galt – Sitten, Anschauungen, Glauben, Moral! Es wäre auch nicht wahr, dass die Frau ein untergeordnetes Geschöpf ist, vorausbestimmt für niedere Lebensfunktionen! Was soll mir das! Jetzt! Was! Ich werfe die Bücher fort und nehme sie wieder auf, allmählich verstehe ich sie besser, und langsam, langsam tut sich mir eine neue fremde Welt auf, wie aus Abendnebeln Sterne tauchen. Und dann wieder habe ich die seltsame Vorstellung, als hätte ich all' die neuen Gedanken, die in den Büchern stehen, schon einmal gehabt, als hätten sie irgendwo verborgen in mir geruht.

Wenn der Glaube an Seelenwanderung nun doch kein leerer Wahn wäre!

Back home. Now it's going to get better, much better. I no longer feel sedated. I'm awake, almost energetic. I'm going out a lot, I go to galleries, to theatres. I'm reading, yes, mainly I read. I had seen some books mentioned in the paper, Russian, French, Scandinavian books which represent an upheaval, a change of minds and of mores and which are supposed to depict life as it really is. As it really is? Would that be worth the effort of depiction? I have read these books for days on end. At times they would seize me to the point of an abnormal excitement, of shuddering sensation. Then I wouldn't understand them anymore. If I tried to hold on to a thought, it would disappear again. I also didn't take the time to read them closely, page by page, I just leafed through the books. I'm running out of time. I want to grasp the soul of everything as it flies by. It's as though I'm being pursued by something that's always right behind me – what? Death, madness, or something else?

A mass movement of ideas, moods and thoughts rushes over me. How? These writers reject what was previously considered irrefutable – customs, views, beliefs, morals! Nor do they believe that woman is a subordinate creature, predestined for the lower functions of life! What is this to me! now! what! I throw the books away and take them up again, gradually I understand them better, and slowly, a new and strange world opens up to me, like stars emerging from the evening mists. And then again I have the strange impression that I had already had all the new thoughts in the books, as if they had been hidden somewhere inside of me.

If only the belief in transmigration were not an empty delusion!

Die Bücher lese ich besonders gern, wo Frauen, von feurigem Idealismus getrieben, Heroisches, Hingebendes vollbringen. Ob ich eine solche Frau hätte werden können, wenn – Und ich war zeitlebens Magd!

* * *

Ich habe etwas Neues in mir entdeckt – Eitelkeit. Ich habe nie gewusst, was Eitelkeit ist. Ich hatte mich so jung verlobt. Eduard hatte keinen Sinn für Äußeres. Er bemerkte gar nicht, ob ich gut oder schlecht aussah. Der einzige Maßstab für meine Kleidung war ihr Billigkeit und Dauerhaftigkeit gewesen, und ob die Stoffe sich wenden ließen. Reizende und anmutige Kostüme fallen mir jetzt auf der Straße in die Augen. Vielleicht ist mein Sinn für Schönes auch geweckt worden durch die vielen Bilder, die ich sehe. Muss ich denn so garstig sein? Ich habe mir ein Kleid von feiner schwarzer Wolle angefertigt, das lang und faltig über die Füße fällt, mit einem Tuch über den Schultern, ganz, wie ich es auf einem Bilde von Marie Antoinette gesehen hatte. Mein graues Haar, das stark ist und ziemlich kurz, ließ ich frei auf die Schulter fallen. Ich dachte auch daran, mir eine Blume, eine unscheinbare, vorzustecken. Ich versuchte es mit einem kleinen Veilchentouffe. Ich warf es gleich wieder fort. Es sah albern aus, als wollte ich jünger erscheinen. Nur das nicht!

Wenn ich nun so in der Dämmerung – es muss dämmerig sein – durch das Zimmer gehe, an dem Spiegel vorbei, dann sehe ich aus, als wäre ich jemand, irgend jemand Anders als die gute Frau Schmidt und gar nicht mehr alt, und mein Herz klopft, und ich blicke um mich, als wollte ich – wenn ich nur wüsste, was? Ich muss zuweilen in mich hineinlachen, als hätte ich Agnes Schmidt überlistet, die fremde Person, die ich sein wollte. Gehe ich bei Tage aus, so ziehe ich meine alten Kleider wieder an und habe dann die Vorstellung, dass ich verkleidet bin, und wenn mich irgend eine alte Bekannte grüßt, wundere ich mich beinahe, wieso sie mich erkannt hat.

I particularly like reading books where women, driven by fiery idealism, perform heroic, self-sacrificing feats. I wonder if I could have become such a woman if – But I was a servant all my life!

* * *

I discovered something new in myself – vanity. I never knew what vanity was. I had gotten engaged so young. Eduard had no sense of appearance. He didn't even notice whether I looked good or bad. The only measure for my clothes had been their cheapness and durability, and whether the fabric could be reused. Now, charming and graceful dresses catch my eye on the street. Perhaps my sense of beauty has also been awakened by the many pictures I see. Do I have to be so terribly ugly? I have made myself a dress of fine black wool that falls long and wrinkled over my feet, with a shawl over my shoulders, just as I had seen in a picture of Marie Antoinette. I let my grey hair, which is thick and relatively short, fall freely onto my shoulders. I also thought about getting a flower, a discreet one, to pin in it. I tried it with a small tuft of violets. I pulled them out again immediately. It looked ridiculous, as if I wanted to appear younger. Anything but that!

If I walk through the room, past the mirror, at dusk – and *only* at dusk – I look as if I am someone, anyone, other than the good Frau Schmidt, and not old at all anymore, and my heart beats, and I look around as if I wanted to – if only I knew what! I have to laugh from time to time, as if I had outwitted Agnes Schmidt, the stranger I was supposed to be. When I go out during the day, I put my old clothes back on and feel as if I'm in disguise, and if an old acquaintance greets me, I almost wonder how they recognized me.

Abends laufe ich oft ohne Hut auf die Straße. Nur ein Tuch um den Kopf. Ich habe jetzt immer, einen Zug, mich von allerhand freizumachen. Ich weiß selbst nicht recht, wovon. Auch von den gehäkelten Deckchen, die sind nun alle fort. Ich habe so viel Blumen, als ich nur konnte, gekauft, starkduftende. Wenn ich dann die Augen zumache, und es duftet so stark, so träume ich all die Märchen nach, die ich in meine Jugend nicht lesen durfte.

Ich hatte früher nie Bildergalerien besucht. Anfangs ging ich betäubt, verwirrt durch die Säle. Erst allmählich fingen die Bilder an auf mich zu wirken, einzelne wenigstens, vor denen ich immer wieder stehen bleibe, zumeist vor Böcklin. Ich liebe die klare Märchenpracht, das Übernatürliche seiner Farben, die goldenen Bäume, die purpurnen Gewänder, den strahlenden Äther, die seligen Blumen. Ja, in diese Natur gehören Götter, Priester und Traumgestalten. Selbst seine Tiere haben einen mystisch träumerischen Zug.

Warum hat Böcklin nicht Lohengrin gemalt in dem Nachen, den die Zauberschwäne ziehen? Warum nicht den Leichenzug Siegfrieds über die Heide hin, Musik ist seine Farbe, bald Schalmeienklang, bald ein Requiem oder ein Choral. Ich komme dahinter, mich fesselt und bewegt nur, was abseits vom Wirklichen liegt. Eine Spannung auf dämmernd Fernes, auf Wunderbares. Oder greife ich vielleicht zu solchen Erregungen, wie der Proletarier zum Alkohol, weil er substantielle Nahrung nicht haben kann? Will ich Rausch?

* * *

In the evening, I often walk down the street without a hat. Just a shawl over my head. I have a constant urge to free myself from all sorts of things. I am not quite sure from what exactly. From the crocheted doilies too, they are all gone now. I bought as many flowers as I could, strongly-scented ones. If I close my eyes, their smell is so strong that I dream of all of the fairytales which I wasn't allowed to read in my youth.

I had never visited art galleries before. At first I wandered, dazed and bewildered, through the halls. Only gradually did the pictures begin to have an effect on me, a select few at least, which I would stop in front of again and again, mostly by Böcklin.[5] I love the lucid fairytale splendour, the hyperrealism of his colours, the golden trees, the crimson walls, the radiant ether, the blissful flowers. This is the natural world of gods, priests, and dream figures. Even the animals have a mystical and dream-like air.

Why didn't Böcklin paint Lohengrin in the boat pulled by the magic swans?[6] Why not Siegfried's funeral procession over the heath, music is its colour, sounding like an oboe at one moment, a requiem or hymn at the next. I follow behind; only that which lies beyond reality captures and moves me. Longing for the distant dusk, for the wonderful. Or perhaps I simply reach for such stimulation as the worker does for alcohol, because he can't get substantial nourishment? Do I want euphoria?

* * *

---

[5] Arnold Böcklin (1827-1901) was a Swiss painter, know for his symbolist works including *The Isle of the Dead* (1880-1886) and *Self-portrait with Death playing the fiddle* (1872) which inspired Romantic artists across Europe.
[6] Lohengrin, son of Percival, is a knight of the Holy Grail and is sent on a quest to rescue a maiden in a boat pulled by a swan. As with the reference to Siegfried, Dohm probably knows the legend from Wagner's opera, *Lohengrin* (1848).

Ich mache weite Spaziergänge. Früher ging ich nur aus, um Besorgungen zu machen. Nun aber gehe ich wirklich spazieren, langsam, durch den Tiergarten. Das Wetter ist seit Tagen schon trüb und regenschwer. Luft und Himmel grau, immer grau. Die noch grünen Blätter verschossen, schwarzfleckig. Der Boden bedeckt mit bräunlichem und schmutziggelbem Laub, dazwischen abgebrochene, morsche Zweige. In der Luft etwas Modriges. Die feuchte, schwere Erde scheint die Blätter in sich zu saugen. Sie nährt sich ja davon. Das ist nun mein Los auch, so abzusterben in Muffigkeit und Grämlichkeit, aufgesogen – –

In einem abgelegenen Teil des Tiergartens ist ein kleiner, wirrer, eingezäunter Garten, ich glaube mit einem Gärtnerhäuschen darin. Neulich war die Tür offen. Ich trat ein. In einer Ecke stand ein morsches Bildwerk von Sandstein, ganz von späten wilden Rosen eingehüllt, rote Rosen, purpurrote. Ich bog die Rosen auseinander, um zu sehen, was das für ein Bildsäule war. Sie hatte keinen Kopf. Die Säule war ganz rot gesprenkelt, als wäre Blut aus dem kopflosen Rumpf daran niedergeträufelt, und davon flammten die Rosen so rot.

Mir war, als wüsste ich, wem der Kopf, der auf der Bildsäule fehlte, gehörte, und ich hätte es nur vergessen. Ich suchte nach dem Kopf in den Gebüschen. Und jedes Mal, wenn ich wieder an die Stelle komme, suche ich unwillkürlich nach dem Kopf. Und unwillkürlich fasse ich nach meinem Kopf. Aber der ist noch da. Nur nicht so recht fest.

Im Tiergarten ist's jetzt so trübe. Ich wollte einen Blick in's Weite, Freie, fernab von der Stadt und von den Menschen. Felder und Wiesen wollte ich.

Von meiner Wohnung ist es nicht weit, bis man auf die Chaussee kommt, die nach Wilmersdorf führt. Dahin ging ich. Ja freies Feld! Auf der einen Seite grünlich graues Erdreich, missfarbige Sandflecken, von kurzen Gräsern durchwachsen, ab und zu ein Büschel Kraut oder ein Kieferstrauch, in der Ferne eine Reihe dünner Bäumchen.

I go on long walks. Before I only went out to run errands. But now I go *walking*, slowly, through the Tiergarten. There have been heavy clouds of rain for days already. Air and sky grey, always grey. The still-green leaves faded, speckled black; the ground covered with brownish yellow foliage, between broken, rotting branches. Something mouldy in the air. The moist, heavy earth seems to absorb the leaves. This is how it feeds itself. This is now my fate as well, to die off in such mustiness and sullenness, absorbed – –

In a small, secluded area of the Tiergarten is an overgrown, enclosed garden, with, I believe, a gardener's hut. One day, the door was open. I went inside. In the corner, there stood a decaying sandstone sculpture, completely enshrouded in withered wild roses, red roses, purpled red roses. I pulled the roses apart from one another, to see what sort of statue it was. She had no head. The sculpture was mottled all over with red, as though blood were dripping from her headless trunk, making the roses blaze so red.

It seemed to me as if I knew who the missing head belonged to, and I had simply forgotten. I looked for the head in the bushes. And every time I come back to this point, I start searching involuntarily for the head. And reaching involuntarily for my own head. But mine is still there. Just not as secure as it should be.

It is so gloomy now in the Tiergarten. I wanted to look out further, into the open, far from the city and its people. I want fields and meadows.

It is not far from my apartment to the road which leads to Wilmersdorf. That's where I went. Yes, an open field! On one side, greenish-grey earth, patches of discoloured sand, interspersed with short grasses, now and again a tuft of herbs or a pine bush, in the distance a row of spindly trees.

Auf der andern Seite, ich weiß nicht, waren es Felder oder Bauplätze oder Ablagerungsstellen für allerhand. Eine fade Luft. Kein frischer Hauch. Gerümpel über das ganze Feld hin verstreut, zerbrochene Gießkannen und alte Stiefel. Düngerhaufen, ein paar Leinewandlappen, Ziegelsteine. An einer andern Stelle Gestrüpp von Kartoffeln und ein Stück Lattenzaun, daneben lila Abhub von verfaulenden Kohlköpfen. Eine Laube aus Brettern, lose zusammengeschlagen, mit etwas schwärzlich schmutzigem Zeug behangen, dahinter eine Sonnenblume. Ein verkrüppelter Baum, unter dem ein morscher Karren stand. Ein Arbeitswagen mit abgezehrten Gäulen, der die letzten Kartoffeln und Kohlköpfe auflud. Braunes Gestrüpp, graues, schwärzliches Gestrüpp, Nebeldunst. In der Ferne die Hinterhäuser von Mietskasernen.

Entnervt, missmutig schlenderte ich die öde, langweilige Straße dahin.

Ein seltsamer Wagen kam mir langsam entgegen, ein kleines Wohnhaus auf Rädern, mit Fenstern auf allen Seiten. An den Fenstern weiße Gardinen und braune Kinderköpfchen, die lustig herauslugten. Zigeuner waren es, die von Ort zu Ort fuhren. Ein kaum erwachsenes, junges Ding kam zu mir herangehüpft und bettelte – nein, sie bettelte nicht, sie redete mir mit schelmischer Anmut zu, ihr etwas zu schenken. Wohin sie führen, fragte ich. Sie lachte und sagte: "Weiter." Ob sie keinen bestimmten Wohnsitz hätten? Sie lachte wieder. In dem Kasten da würden sie geboren, darin heirateten sie, kriegten Kinder, und darin stürben sie immer unterwegs.

Und dieses Mädchen, das eine Art Ballkleid mit Volants trug, vom Kehricht aufgelesen, tanzte vor mir her, in blühender Lebenslust, in jeder Bewegung Schönheit und Anmut. Nichts Dumpfes und Stumpfes in diesen Zigeunern. Ob es die unbändige Freiheit ist, in der sie leben, der sie diese geschmeidige Grazie, die fröhliche Sicherheit ohne Menschenfurcht verdanken? Ob das das Richtige ist? Immer weiter, von Ort zu Ort, jede Nacht wo anders schlafen, heut auf luftigen Höhen, morgen im Dunkel des Waldes, auf breiten sonnigen Ebenen, am Ufer der Flüsse, im Schoß der Berge!

On the other side, I don't know if they were fields or building sites or dumbing grounds for all sorts of things. A stale air. Not a hint of freshness. Rubbish was strewn across the entire field, broken watering cans and old boots. Piles of fertiliser, a couple of linen tapestries, bricks. In another place, scrubs of potatoes and a piece of picket fence, next to it a purple heap of rotting cabbages. An arch made of boards, loosely knocked together, hung with something blackish and dirty; behind it, a sunflower. A stunted tree, under which stood a rotten cart. A work wagon with worn-out legs, which was loaded with the last potatoes and cabbages. Brown undergrowth, grey, black shrubbery, misty haze. In the distance, the rear buildings of apartment blocks.

I skulked along the dull, boring street, exasperated and disgruntled.

A strange carriage came slowly towards me, a small house on wheels, with windows on all sides. The windows had white curtains, and the brown heads of children peeked out merrily. They were 'Zigeuner', who travelled from place to place. A barely grown-up thing came skipping up to me and begged – no, she didn't beg, she asked me with mischievous charm, to give her a little something. I asked where they were going. She laughed and said, 'Further.' Did they have no real home? She laughed again. They were born in the cart, were married in it, bore children in it and they died in it, all whilst on the road.

And this girl, who wore a kind of flounced ballgown picked up from the rubbish, danced in front of me, full of joie de vivre, beauty and grace in her every movement. Nothing dumpy or stumpy about these 'Zigeuner'. Is it the unbridled freedom in which they live that gives them this supple grace, this cheerful confidence without fear of man? Is it the right thing to do? Always on, from place to place, sleeping somewhere different every night, today on airy heights, tomorrow in the darkness of the forest, on broad sunny plains, on the banks of rivers, in the lap of the mountains!

Es hat mitunter etwas Schreckliches, die Vorstellung, immer auf einem, einem Punkt bleiben zu müssen, während es Millionen schönere Punkte gibt. Sie nie zu sehen! Armselig sind wir organisiert. So ganz ohne Flügel.

Unwillkürlich ging ich, so schnell ich konnte, weiter – weiter!

Ich kam in die Nähe des Grunewalds, wo am Rand eines dürftigen Kiefernwäldchens eine Reihe Wirtshäuser stehen. Leute aus dem kleinen Bürgerstand pflegen da einzukehren.

Vor dem Gehölz war eine Wiese, von Streifen welken Kartoffelkrauts unterbrochen. Durch das dünne Gras blickte das schwarze feuchte Erdreich. Ab und zu kleine Haufen von Scherben und Kehricht. Neubauten noch mit dem Gerüst. In der Ferne die Häusermassen der Stadt. Es war Sonntag. Ich hatte nicht daran gedacht. Schlächter- und Bäcker-Equipagen mit zahlreicher Familie hielten vor den Wirtshäusern. Junge Leute tummelten sich auf der Wiese, spielten Reifen und Haschens, die jungen Mädchen mit wallendem Haar, in hellen Kleidern von grellen Farben, viel Himmelblau und Rosa. Auf einem Steinhaufen saßen die Eltern und aßen Butterbrote, die sie ihren Kobern entnahmen. Die Mütter hatten Federn oder bunte Blumen auf den Hüten, neben sich ein Häkel- oder Strickzeug. Hinter ihnen Regenschirme. Um sie herum fettige Papiere. In den Restaurants: Schnellphotographen, Schießstände, Leierkasten und Karussells. In einem Garten produzierte sich ein Bär. Trübe, schwer, vornehm hing der Herbsthimmel über der grellen Vergnügtheit.

Das unablässige Knallen der Gewehre, der Geruch des Bieres, der Leierkasten, der immer leidenschaftlicher spielte, die Karussellpferdchen, die immer wilder mit den lustigen Reiterinnen dahinsprengten, das Gekreisch über den Bären – war das nicht wüst, sinnlos! Und so nah dem Staub der Landstraße und ohne Sonne!

There is something terrible about the idea of always having to stay in one place, when there are millions of more beautiful places. Never to see them! We are poorly organised. So completely without wings.

Involuntarily, I walked on as fast as I could – onwards! Onwards!

I came near the Grunewald, where a row of inns stood on the edge of a sparse pine grove. People from the lower middle classes tend to stop off there.

In front of the wood there was a meadow, cut across by stripes of limp stems. There were glimpses of the damp black earth through the thin grass. Little piles of broken glass and litter here and there. New buildings, already rusting. The city's mass of houses in the distance. It was a Sunday. I hadn't thought about it. Butcher and baker carts with their large families stopped outside the pubs. Young people were running about in the meadow, playing tag and with hoops, the young girls with flowing hair, in bright, colourful dresses, lots of sky blues and pinks. The parents were sitting on a pile of rocks and eating buttered bread which they took out of their baskets. The mothers had feathers or bright flowers on their hats, next to them a bit of crochet or knitting. Behind them, umbrellas. Greasy papers around them. In the restaurants: photographers, shooting galleries, barrel organs, and carousels. In a garden, a bear was performing. Dull and heavy, the autumn sky hung nobly over the garish merriment.

The incessant sounding of guns, the smell of beer, the barrel organs being played ever more fervently, the carousel ponies galloping ever more wildly with their jocular riders, the shrieks about the bear – how hollow, senseless! And so near the dust of the road and without any sun!

Was brauchen sie Sonne! Jugend ist ja Sonne. Und das Alter – seine milde, klare Ruhe nicht auch Sonne? Sonne im Winter. Sie wärmt nicht. Ich will wirkliche Sonne, südliche Sonne, Sommersonne. Ich will – Still! Still! Alte Mignon! In Berlin, in einer hässlichen, sonnenlosen Straße hast du gelebt, und da wirst du bleiben und sterben.

Fröstelnd, geringschätzig wandte ich mich von der kreischenden Lustigkeit ab. Hinter mir her rief ein junger Bursche: "Na, junge Frau, wie geht's?" Ausgelassenes Gelächter.

Ich merke, dass ich zuweilen den Spott der Menschen errege, und weiß nicht, wodurch. Es irritiert mich. Ich leide unter der geheimen Angst, man könne das Widersprechende zwischen meinem Inneren und meinem Äußeren merken. Sie haben ja dekretiert, wie der Mensch in jedem Lebensalter sein soll. Darum, wenn ich Leute kommen sehe, krümme ich mich zusammen, damit ich noch älter erscheine, als ich bin. Ich gebe mir ein stumpfes Ansehen, als vegetierte ich nur so hin, wie es meinen Jahren zukommt. *Der* Alte ist eine liebenswürdige Vorstellung, *die* Alte eine unangenehme. Will man Jemand recht bitter kränken, so sagt man: Du bist ein altes Weib.

Ein alter Mann, ist er weise, kenntnisreich, gut, edelsinnig, er wird nach seinem Wert geschätzt. Gedankentiefe Sprüche, und wären sie in Runenschrift in uralten Stein gehauen, sie gelten voll nach ihrem Inhalt. Spräche und dächte aber eine lebendige alte Frau das Weiseste und Edelste, es wäre in den Wind gesprochen. Und wer freundlich über sie urteilt, sagt: schade, dass sie nicht jünger ist.

Ist das nicht ohne Scham, dass man die edelsten Eigenschaften beim Weibe nur als eine Würze ihres jungen Leibes gelten lässt?

So geringschätzig, so widerwillig blickt man auf die Alte, als wäre ihr Alter eine Schuld, die Strafe verdiente. Ihr Jungen und Jüngeren, Ihr werdet doch auch alt, und Ihr wollt alt werden, und Ihr haltet es für ein grausames Geschick, nicht alt zu werden.

Warum widersprecht Ihr Euch so?

But what would they need of the sun! Youth itself is the sun. And age – is its mild, clear quiet not also sun? Sun in winter. Sun that doesn't warm. I want the real sun, southern sun, summer sun. I want – Quiet! quiet! old Mignon! In Berlin, in a horrible, sunless street you have lived, and there you will stay and die.

Shivering, contemptuous, I turned away from the shrill happiness. Behind me a young boy called 'Hey, little miss, how's it going?'. Uproarious laughter.

I have noticed that I sometimes provoke mockery from people, and I don't know why. It irritates me. I suffer from concealed dread that one can see the contradiction between my inner self and my outward appearance. The correct behaviour for each age has already been decreed. So when I see people coming towards me, I crumple in on myself, so I appear even older than I am. I give myself a dulled appearance, as though I was just vegetating, as befits my age. The old *man* is an agreeable image, the old *woman* is a repulsive one. If you really want to insult someone, tell them: you're an old lady.

An old man is wise, knowledgeable, good, sensible, he is recognised for his worth, for his profound utterances, which could be engraved as runes in ancient stone and still valued for their content. But if a living old woman were to speak and think the wisest and most noble things, it would be like words spoken into the wind. And those who judge her kindly can only say: 'It's a shame she isn't younger'.

Is it not shameful to consider a woman's noblest qualities to be merely the remnants of her younger body?

The old woman is looked upon with such contempt, such reluctance, as if her age were a fault which ought to be punished. All of you, young and younger still, you will grow old too and you'll want to grow old, and you'll consider it a cruel fate not to grow old.

So why contradict yourselves?

Existiert denn der Mensch nur für einen bestimmten Lebensabschnitt? Ist die Kindheit nur Ouvertüre, das Alter nur Epilog? Nein doch. Auch die Kindheit, auch das Alter haben volles, ganzes Daseinsrecht. Ein Mensch, und wäre es auch nur ein Weib, und wäre das Weib achtzig Jahre alt, er ist in seinem achtzigsten Jahr ebenso lebensberechtigt wie in seinem zwanzigsten. Wisst Ihr denn, ob er in seinem achtzigsten nicht mehr wert ist, als er es in seinem zwanzigsten war?

In der Antipathie gegen alte Frauen ist viel von der Barbarei früherer Zeitalter, von Zeitaltern, in denen auch die Krankheit als eine Schuld galt, und wo man die Alten, wenn sie nichts mehr leisteten, einfach ersäufte.

Gibt es keinen Heiligen, dem wir unsere Not an's Herz legen können?

Heilige Zukunft! Du, tu Fürbitte für uns alte Weiber!

* * *

Wie einsam ich bin. Soweit meine Gedanken reichen, kein Mensch, der für mich da ist.

Aber ich will ja einsam sein. Ich fühle mich ernüchtert, herabgezogen, sobald ich Stimmen oder Schritte von Menschen höre, und warte ungeduldig, bis sie sich in der Ferne verloren haben.

Nein, ich kann nie wieder unter Menschen gehen. Ich dämmere wieder tagelang so hin. Und plötzlich fahre ich dann mit nervösem Zittern aus meinen wachen Träumen auf. Aber ich leide ja, ich leide! Ist das der Lohn für die Bravheit eines ganzen Lebens?

War ich denn wirklich so brav und pflichtgetreu? Ich hätte ja gar nicht anders sein können! Ich war vielleicht nur deshalb so zahm, weil man mich von Kindheit an gezähmt hatte.

Do you mean to say that we only exist for a specific fragment of our lives? Is childhood just the overture, old age the epilogue? No, it's not. Children, the elderly – both have a full and complete right to existence. Any person, even if that person were only a woman and that woman were eighty years old, is just as worthy of living at eighty as they are at twenty. In fact, how do you know that they're not worth more at eighty than they are at twenty?

Much of the barbarism of days gone by can be found in this antipathy towards old women, when sickness was a fault, and the elderly were simply drowned when they were no longer of any use.

Is there no saint to whom we can entrust our plight?

O holy future! I beg of you, intercede on behalf of us old women!

* * *

How lonely I am. As far as my thoughts span, there is no one there for me.

But I want to be lonely, I do. I feel disillusioned, weighed down, as soon as I hear people's voices, their steps, and wait impatiently until they get lost in the distance.

No, I cannot go on among these people. And so, day after day, I drift away. Then suddenly I wake from my lucid dreams with a nervous shiver. But I'm suffering, yes, I'm suffering! Is that the price for a lifetime of goodness?

Was I really so well-behaved and dutiful? I could hardly have been any different! Perhaps I was only so tame because I had been tamed since childhood.

Ich sah einmal auf einer abseits gelegenen Chaussee, in der Nähe eines Wärterhäuschens, auf einer weiten Strecke entlang, Bäume in allen möglichen und unmöglichen Formen. Der Bahnwärter hatte in seinen Mußestunden künstliche Drahtgestelle angefertigt, in die er die Bäumchen hineinwachsen ließ. Da sah man eine Leier, einen Stuhl, eine Krone, einen Adler und zahllose, andere Gegenstände. Ich wollte darüber lachen. Ehe ich aber zum Lachen kam, wurde ich nachdenklich. Ein fertiges Gestell, in das hineinzuwachsen man die Bäume zwang. Wie vollkommen war das Kunststück gelungen. Ob Bäume, ob Menschen, das Kunststück wird immer gelingen. Dressur! Der Schäferhund und der Ziehhund, die sind auch brav und pflichtgetreu.

Man hatte meine Natur an die Kette gelegt. Nun bin ich losgelassen, und ich irre in der neuen, fremden Welt umher und würde vielleicht Unheil anrichten, aber da ist schon eine neue Kette – das Alter.

Für Andere leben, das soll das Richtige, das Wahre sein. Wäre es so, und Jeder lebte für den Andern, so hätten doch auch Andere für mich leben müssen, und es wäre dann doch dasselbe und viel einfacher, wenn Jeder gleich für sich selbst lebte. Eine Mutter soll nur für die Kinder da sein! So soll ich nur leben und arbeiten für die Tochter, und die Tochter soll wieder nur für ihre Kinder da sein. Welch ein sinnloser, unfruchtbarer Kreislauf.

Hatte ich wirklich nur Pflichten gegen Andere, keine gegen mich? Waren all die Anderen mehr als ich? Wären sie's gewesen, dann – – dann freilich – –

Hatte Eduard ein Recht zu sagen: lebe für mich! Hatten es meine Eltern? Meine Kinder? Hätte ich die Pflicht gegen mich erfüllt und meine Intelligenz entwickelt, so wären an meiner geklärten Vernunft meine Kinder im Denken fortgeschritten, und sie wären nicht wieder geworden, wie ich war. Unsere Pflichten! Müssten sie nicht in der Richtung liegen, die uns besser, edler macht, nicht umgekehrt? Dürfen sie uns auf ein niedrigeres Niveau herabdrücken?

Once, tucked away behind one of the watch houses, I saw trees in all sorts of possible and impossible shapes, stretching along an endless alley. During his breaks, the signalman had made artificial wire frames for the saplings to grow into. A lyre, a chair, a crown, an eagle, and countless other objects. It made me want to laugh. But before I could, I grew thoughtful. A completed frame into which trees were forced to grow. How perfectly the feat had been accomplished. Be it with trees or with people, this feat is always accomplished. Dressage! The sheep dog and the draft dog are just as well-behaved and dutiful as we are.

My Self had been put on a chain. Now I have been set free, and I wander around the new, strange world and might have caused mischief, except there is already a new chain – old age.

Living for others: that's supposed to be the correct way, the genuine way to live. If it were truly so, and everyone lived for others, then others would also have to live for me, and it would be just the same and much easier if everyone lived for themselves in the first place. A mother should only be there for her children! So I should live and work only for my daughter, and in turn my daughter should only be there for her children. What an absurd, fruitless cycle!

Did I really just have duties towards others, none towards myself? Were all the others worth more than me? If they had been, then – – then of course – –

Did Eduard have a right to say: live for me! Did my parents? my children? If I had fulfilled my duty to myself and developed my intelligence, then my children would have benefited from my illuminated reason, and they wouldn't have turned out like I did. Our duties! Do they not have to lie in a direction which makes us better, more noble, rather than the other way around? Can they press us down to a lower level?

Vieles, was man uns als Pflicht einprägt, ist ganz gewiss nicht unsere Pflicht, z.B. die Pflicht, dem Gatten anzugehören, auch wenn unsere Natur sich dagegen auflehnt. Und wenn das eine falsche Pflicht ist, warum nicht auch vieles Andere, das man im Namen der Pflicht von uns fordert.

Liebe deinen Nächsten wie dich selbst, heißt's im Evangelium.

Ich darf, ich soll mich also selbst lieben? Was habe ich mir denn zu Liebe getan? Nichts, das ich wüsste.

Ich war doch aber immer zufrieden? Ich? Aber ich war ja gar kein Ich. Agnes Schmidt! Ein Name! Eine Hand, ein Fuß, ein Leib! Keine Seele, kein Hirn. Ich habe ein Leben gelebt, wo ich gar nicht dabei war.

Ist das ganz wahr? Es gab doch so schöne Momente in meinem Leben, als die Kinder klein waren, so süß Geschöpfe.

Nun aber sind sie doch gar nicht mehr meine Kinder, sie sind die Frauen ihrer Männer. Sie haben sich von mir fort verloren.

Vielleicht kommt all' meine innere Not daher, dass mein Vater Kanzleirat war und meine Mutter Kanzleirätin, und dass ich einige Tropfen Eisen zu wenig im Blut hatte, und das ärmliche Blut konnte die Gehirnnerven nicht bewegen.

Wer und was bin ich eigentlich? Ich bin neugierig auf mich.

Es ist mir oft, als ob Funken mich berührten von irgend einem Feuer, einer Sonne, die ich nicht sehe. Ich blase in die Funken mit aller Kraft, damit sie Flamme werden. Mein Atem ist so kurz. Sie verglimmen die Funken – Asche.

* * *

Much of what we are taught is our duty is quite certainly not, such as the duty of belonging to one's husband, even when our nature revolts against it. And if that is a false duty, why not many of the other things that are demanded from us in the name of duty, too?

Love thy neighbour as thyself, so it says in the Evangelium.

So I am allowed, I am supposed to love myself? What have I done out of love for myself? nothing that I'm aware of.

Yet I had always been satisfied? I? but I was no 'I'. Agnes Schmidt! a name! a hand, a foot, a body! no soul, no brain. I've lived a life in which I wasn't even present.

Is that completely true? There had been such beautiful moments in my life, after all, when the children were small – such sweet creatures.

But now they aren't even my children anymore; they are the wives of their husbands. They were taken away from me.

Perhaps all of my inner distress comes from the fact that my father was a clerk, and my mother was the wife of a clerk, and that I had a few drops too little iron in my blood, and this poor blood couldn't stir my cranial nerves.

Who and what am I really? I am curious about myself.

I often feel as if I were being touched by the sparks from some fire, a sun which I cannot see. I blow into the sparks with all my strength so that they become flames. My breath is so short. The sparks fade away – ashes.

★ ★ ★

Heut hatte ich düstere Momente, Gedanken an Unheilvolles, an Tod. Die vielen Blumen im Zimmer, halb verwelkt, hauchten einen faden, abgestorbenen Geruch aus. Ich hatte lange gelesen, Alles durcheinander, Philosophisches, Naturwissenschaftliches, und hatte mich abgemartert, aus dem Chaos klare Gedankenbilder zu sondern.

Alles still um mich her. Nur das Ticken der Uhr. Es wurde dunkel im Zimmer – Nacht. Von der Straßenlaterne her fiel ein matter Lichtstreifen über den niedrigen, weißen Ofen, auf dem eine Vase steht. Er sah wie eine Graburne aus.

Ich hatte kürzlich ein Bild gesehen: ein Mensch im Sarge. Er hat den Sargdeckel gehoben und starrt mit stierem Entsetzen empor. Schauerlich! Wird er die Kraft haben, den Deckel ganz zu heben, und aus dem Sarg zu steigen, oder – er fällt – fällt – –

Solch ein Gefühl hatte ich, als läge ich im Sarge und sähe zwischen dem erhobenen Deckel hindurch ein Stückchen Himmels, ein kleines Stück, und in der unaussprechlichen Sehnsucht, den ganzen, weiten Horizont mit meinem Augen zu umspannen, stieß ich und stieß gegen den Deckel. Und ich fühlte, meine Kraft erlahmte, meine Gedanken versagten, und langsam, langsam – der Sargdeckel – er fiel – fiel – – In furchtbarer Angst sprang ich auf, ich nahm ein Tuch um den Kopf und stürzte hinaus. Ein frischer, klarer Dezemberabend.

Ja, das beruhigte, der weite, große Sternenhimmel über mir. Nun wunderte ich mich fast über den Schauder in uns, heimzugehen, uns aufzulösen in's unermesslich Ewige. Was ist denn in mir, das wert wäre, durch Ewigkeiten zu sein! Lass ruhig den Deckel fallen, alte Frau!

* * *

Today I had dark moments, ominous thoughts, thoughts of death. The many flowers in the room, half-wilted, exhaled a stale, dead smell. I had been reading for a long time, everything mixed up, philosophical, scientific books, and had exhausted myself trying to extract clear mental images out of the chaos.

Everything around me is still. Only the ticking of the clock. The darkened room – night. From the streetlamp, a dull streak of light fell over the low, white stove on which a vase stood. It looked like a funeral urn.

I recently saw a picture of a man in a coffin. He has lifted the lid of the coffin and stares up in stunned horror. Gruesome! Will he have the strength to lift the lid completely and get out of the coffin, or – he's falling – falling – –?

I felt as if I were lying in the coffin and could see a piece of the heavens, a small piece, up through the raised lid, and with unspeakable longing to encompass the whole, wide horizon with my eyes, I pushed and pushed against the lid. And I felt my strength fail, my thoughts fail, and slowly, slowly – the coffin lid – it fell – fell – – In terrible fear I jumped up, I wrapped a scarf over my head and rushed out. A fresh, clear December evening.

Yes, that was reassuring, the wide, great starry sky above me. Now I almost wonder why we shudder at the thought of going home, of dissolving into immeasurable eternity. What is there in me that is worthy of existing for eternity? Let the lid fall, old woman!

* * *

Draußen im Freien finde ich Ruhe. Sobald ich zwischen meinen vier Wänden bin, fängt es wieder an, das Wirre, die Empfindung, als säße der Kopf nur so locker auf. Und ich halte ihn zuweilen, ich halte ihn mit beiden Händen. Ich kann nicht denken, was und wie ich will. Es ist, als drängen Ideen, Bilder, Vorstellungen von außen auf mich ein, heiße und wilde, zu viele! zu viele! Der Raum in Gehirn ist zu eng. Sie ersticken sich gegenseitig. Ich fühle ihre Zuckungen. Todeszuckungen? Um wahnsinnig zu werden.

Wahnsinn – ist das etwas Anderes, als das Stillhalten den Ideen, Visionen, die zu uns kommen und von uns gehen, wir wissen nicht, woher und wohin, und über die wir keine Macht haben?

Ist das Wahnsinn, so war ich länger als fünfzig Jahre wahnsinnig. Immer habe ich fremdem Willen, fremder Meinung still gehalten. Nach dem Naturgesetz der Schwere fällt der Apfel bis zum Mittelpunkt der Erde, wenn er keinen Widerstand findet. So scheint es auch ein Naturgesetz, dass der Wille und die Macht der Andern über uns erst eine Grenze an unserem Widerstand finden. Ich war ein Mechanismus, den fremde Mächte in Bewegung setzten. Und nun ringe ich mich von diesem Wahnsinn los. Ich ringe, ringe um meinen Willen, um mein Selbst, um mein Ich.

* * *

I find peace out in the open. As soon as I'm back between my four walls, it starts again, the confusion, the feeling that my head is just sitting there loosely. And I hold it at times, I hold it with both hands. I can't think what I want and how I want. It's as if ideas, images, notions from outside are pressing in on me, hot and wild, too many! too many! The space in my brain is too small. They suffocate each other. I feel their twitches. Twitches of death? They're going to drive me mad.

Madness – is that something different from accepting the ideas, visions that come to us and go from us, we don't know where from or where to, and over which we have no power?

If this is madness, then I have been mad for more than fifty years. I have always accepted the wills and opinions of others. According to the natural law of gravity, the apple falls to the centre of the earth if it finds no resistance. Similarly, it seems to be a law of nature that the will and the power of others over us only find a limit in our resistance. I was a mechanism set in motion by the hands of others. And now I am struggling to free myself from this madness. I am struggling, struggling for my Will, for my Self, for my Soul.

* * *

Wieder seit vier Wochen nicht geschrieben. So Unerwartetes hat sich ereignet. Eine alte Verwandte, von der ich Jahrzehnte nichts gehört, ist gestorben und hat mir 10.000 Mark vermacht. 10.000 Mark! Eine so große Summe! Ich gebe sie Magdalenens Mann. Er kann sie so gut gebrauchen, und er hängt so sehr am Gelde. Gewiss, gern die paar armen Jahre, die ich noch zu leben habe. Ja, das will ich tun. Das ist recht gehandelt.

Andern Glück bereiten, das ist das Beste. Ich habe ja sonst nichts, womit ich Glück bereiten könnte.

Acht Tage später. Nein, ich gebe Eugen das Geld nicht. Ich habe gekämpft und gekämpft. Nun bin ich entschlossen. Ich behalte es. Für mich will ich es verwenden, für mich ganz allein.

Ich will reisen, weit fort! Ja die weite, weite Welt! Der Druck auf meinem Gehirn wird weichen. Ich verheimliche das Geld vor meinen Kindern. Das Meer will ich sehen! Wie ich es lieben werde, das Meer, das große Meer. Und dann – dann – Italien!

Ich kenne ja nur sonnenlose Tage und lange, lange Abende bei Petroleumlicht. Nie mit offenen Augen habe ich Morgen- und Abendröten gesehen, nie – –

Ob es sehr Unrecht ist, dass ich das Geld behalte? Will ich denn Glück? Lust? ja – ein wenig. Aber hauptsächlich will ich vorwärts – aufwärts! Die kleine Hausfrauenseele loswerden, einen Schimmer erhaschen von der großen Weltseele. Eine ethische Wanderlust ist's – – Wirklich? Es ist doch etwas Böses dabei, ich weiß es. Eine Art Rache, um des Unrechts willen, das mir geschehen. Rache? an wem? Ich tat ja Alles freiwillig, Niemand zwang mich. Unkenntnis der Gesetze schützt im bürgerlichen Leben vor Strafe nicht. So, scheint es, ist es auch auf dem Gebiet des Seelenlebens. Ich kannte die Gesetze meiner Natur nicht und verstieß dagegen. Und die Strafe: lebenslänglicher Kerker? Nein, ich will hinaus! Nur ein paar Tropfen aus dem Becher, der den Durst nach Leben stillt, die letzten Tropfen.

Didn't write for another four weeks. Something unexpected happened. An old relative I hadn't heard from in decades died and left me 10,000 Marks. 10,000 Marks! Such a large sum! I'm giving it to Magdalene's husband. He could get such good use out of it, and he is very attached to money. He would, of course, be thankful for it too. Maybe then he would be happy to indulge me for the few pathetic years I have left to live. Yes, that's what I want to do. That would be the right way to handle it.

It's best I try to make other people happy. I have no other means of giving happiness.

Eight days later. No, I'm not giving Eugen the money. I have struggled and struggled. But now I'm resolute. I'm keeping it. I will use it for myself, for me and me alone.

I want to travel far away! Into the wide, wide world! The pressure on my mind will ease. I will conceal the money from my children. I want to see the sea! Oh, how I will love it, the sea, the great sea! And then – then – Italy!

I've only ever known sunless days and long, long evenings by kerosene lights. Never have I seen dusks and dawns with open eyes, never – –

Is it really wrong that I'm keeping the money? Do I want happiness? Delight? yes – a little bit. But mainly I want to move forwards, upwards! To shed the tiny housewife's soul, to grasp a glimmer of the great world's soul. It's pure-hearted wanderlust – – Really? No, there's something evil in it, I know it. A kind of vengeance for the injustice committed against me. Vengeance? on whom? I did everything willingly, no one forced me. Ignorance of the law doesn't protect one from punishment in civil life. It seems the same applies in the life of the soul. I didn't know the laws of my nature and trespassed against them. And the punishment: lifelong imprisonment? No, I want out! Just a few drops from the cup that quenches the thirst for life, the last few drops.

Morgen schon – *morgen.*

Acht Tage später. Ich bin noch immer hier. Ja, etwas Böses ist dabei. Ich werde es nicht los. Mein Gewissen – –

Oder haben wir vielleicht nur Gewissensbisse, wenn wir etwas tun, was im Widerspruch steht mit dem, was die allgemeine Meinung für gut hält. Warum hätten wir sonst so selten ein böses Gewissen wegen schlechter Gedanken, sondern immer nur wegen schlechter Handlungen? Warum schlägt dem das Gewissen nicht, der im Duell einen Menschen tötet, und er wusste vielleicht, dass er besser schoss als sein Gegner. Das war doch Mord. Weil die Andern es aber nicht für Mord halten, sondern für ganz erlaubt, so bleibt auch sein Gewissen stumm.

Es gibt doch aber Gewissen, die feiner und schärfer organisiert sind, und die sich von dem Kollektivgewissen der großen Menge freimachen? Z. B. eine Frau, die in einer erniedrigenden Ehe mit einem schlechten Manne lebt und die mutig dem Manne ihrer Liebe folgt, trotzdem sie den Gatten nicht bewegen kann, in die Scheidung zu willigen. Diese Frau hätte sicher kein schlechtes Gewissen. Aber sie würde doch immer noch mit einer sittlichen Elite übereinstimmen. Oder Charlotte Corday. Die allgemeine Meinung brandmarkte ihre Tat als Mord, eine fanatische Gemeinde aber spricht sie als Heldin frei.

Wenn ich aber etwas täte, das ich für das Richtige hielte und wobei ich ganz, völlig allein stände? Z. B. wenn ich Magdalene klar machte, dass ihr Mann eine niedrige Gesinnung habe und sie verschlechtere, und ich verlangte von ihr, dass sie ihn verließe, und sie täte es und geriet darüber in äußere und innere Not – würde neben der allgemeinen Verurteilung nicht auch mein eigenes Gewissen gegen mich sein? Und das Gewissen wäre doch in diesem Falle ein falscher Name für die Sehnsucht zurück nach den Fleischtöpfen Ägyptens.

Maybe tomorrow – *tomorrow.*

Eight days later. I'm still here. Yes, there's something evil in it. I can't get rid of it. My conscience – –

Or maybe we only have twinges of conscience when we're doing something that stands in opposition to what the general opinion considers good. Why else would we have a guilty conscience because of bad behaviour but rarely because of bad thoughts? Why does a guilty conscience not strike he who kills someone in a duel, even when he knows he is better at shooting than his opponent? It was murder after all. But because others don't consider it murder, but rather entirely permissible, his conscience stays equally silent.

Yet are there consciences which have a more delicate and sharp constitution, and so are set free from the collective conscience of the masses? For instance, a woman finds herself in a degrading marriage with a bad man and bravely pursues her love for another, even though she is unable to persuade her husband to agree to divorce. Such a woman surely wouldn't have a bad conscience. And still, she'd adhere to the ideals of a moral elite. Or Charlotte Corday.[7] General consensus branded her actions as murder, but a fanatical following absolves her as a heroine.

But what if I did something which I thought was right and in which I was completely and utterly alone? For instance, if I made it clear to Magdalene that her low-minded husband was bringing her down, if I urged her to leave him, and she did so, only for her to fall into both physical and mental distress as a result – along with public condemnation, would my own conscience not turn against me too? But conscience, in that case, would just be a false name for a longing to return to the fleshpots of Egypt.[8]

---

[7] Charlotte Corday was a figure of the French revolution who was found guilty of assassinating revolutionary and Jacobin leader Jean-Paul Marat on 13th July 1793.
[8] The 'fleshpots of Egypt' is a reference to Exodus 16:3 where the Israelites in the desert regret leaving the abundance of Egypt where they were enslaved.

Ich behalte das Geld, ich reise.

Ganz gewiss, nicht nur auf ferne Länder ist mein Sinn und Sehnen gerichtet, mehr noch, viel mehr auf ferne Gedanken, Gedanken in der Höhe. Ich sehne mich unaussprechlich nach Weisheit, nach reiner Vernunft, nach Erkenntnis. Alle Gedanken möchte ich denken, alle Gefühle fühlen. Und es ist ein Riegel vor meinem Hirn. Was für eine schaudernd erhabene Lust muss es sein, Gedanken auf Gedanken türmen, bis sie buchstäblich die Sterne berühren und die Welträtsel.

Muss man sich wie Faust immer dem Teufel verschreiben, um zu erkennen? Warum kann man sich nicht dem Himmel verschreiben?

Kürzlich – schreibe ich es? – habe ich Champagner getrunken, heimlich, bei verschlossener Tür. Ich wollte mir Kraft, Gehirnkraft trinken.

Umsonst! Ich bleibe unten.

Denken! Ich habe ja nicht gelernt, zu denken, und das muss man doch lernen. Ich weiß ja nicht, was vor mir gedacht worden ist. Wenn ich meine, hochgekommen zu sein, bin ich immer erst da, wo Andere lange, lange vor mir gestanden haben. Ich kann nicht reden. Aber schreiben? Das Schreiben ist mir natürlich, als hätte ich von Jugend an nichts Anderes getan. Ideen, Bilder drängen sich zu mir, in wirrer Fülle. Und doch – ich kann auch nicht schreiben, was ich schreiben möchte. Das macht, weil ich nicht einmal halb, kaum viertelgebildet bin. Ich will andere höherstrebende Worte, feiner gegliederte Sätze, sie sind da, in meinem Kopfe – eingeschlossen. Ich rüttle, rüttle – umsonst, der Riegel weicht nicht.

Und die Ideen, sie kommen in Nebel und Dunst verhüllt, verschwommen, aphoristische Schatten. Sonne fehlt ihnen, Helle. Alles ist nur Intuition, Augenblicksverstand. Blitz und Finsternis.

I'll keep the money, I'll travel.

Certainly, my mind longs not just for far-flung lands, but also, and to a greater extent, for far-flung thoughts, thoughts of a higher realm. I long indescribably for wisdom, for pure reason, for knowledge. I long to think all thoughts, feel all feelings. And it's a bolt across my brain. What a shudderingly sublime pleasure must it be to pile thought upon thought until they, quite literally, touch the stars, the mysteries of the world.

Must we, like Faust,[9] sign a pact with the devil to possess such knowledge? Why can we not sign a pact with heaven?

Recently – am I really writing this? – I drank champagne, in secret, behind closed doors. I wanted to drink up strength, strength for the brain.

Alas! I remain down below.

Think! I have not yet learned to think and that must be learned. I don't know what has already been thought. When I think I've emerged, I only find myself where others have stood long, long before me. I cannot speak. But write? Writing comes naturally to me, as if I've done nothing else since the days of my youth. Ideas, images flood over me in confused abundance. And yet – I also cannot write what I want to write. Because I don't have half, not even a quarter, of an education. I long for words which aspire to something higher, sentences more finely articulated, they are there in my head – locked up. I shake, shake – alas, the bolt does not budge.

And the ideas, they emerge shrouded in mist and haze, blurred, aphoristic shadows. They lack sun, brightness. It's all just intuition, momentary understanding. Lightning and darkness.

---

[9] The myth of Faust is that of a scholar dissatisfied by his never-ending quest for knowledge and who makes a pact with the devil, exchanging his soul for knowledge and material gain.

Wie mir, so muss einem Stummen sein, der im höchsten Affekt sprechen will, sprechen, und er kann nicht, kann nicht.

Und Keiner hilft mir, Keiner. Ich bin allein.

Die Wissenden, sie haben Lehr- und Wanderjahre gehabt, sie haben Länder und Menschen erforscht, sie haben ganze Bibliotheken studiert, sie haben an den Lippen weiser Lehrer gehangen. Stufe für Stufe muss erklimmen, wer auf die Höhe will, und Führer muss er haben. Fliegen wollen ohne Flügel: Widersinn! Größenwahn!

Oder doch kein Widersinn? Könnte man absehen von Allem, was bisher gedacht wurde, und hinweg über alle Generationen bahnbrechender Geister aus dem Urgrund der eigenen Seele schöpferische Gedanken zeugen? Ich habe es versucht. Über den Zweck unseres Daseins habe ich gesonnen und gesonnen, und nichts gefunden als den Gemeinplatz, dass der Mensch keinen anderen Zweck hat, haben kann, als der Stein, die Pflanze, die Erde: zu werden, zu wachsen, zu vergehen.

Freilich, ja, die Pflanze ist mehr als der Stein, das Tier ist mehr als die Pflanze, der Mensch als das Tier, aber nicht viel mehr, nicht viel.

Und könnte ich auch erkennen und finden, was die Besten der Zeit erkannt und gefunden, es wäre mir nicht genug, nicht genug.

Wie weit kann selbst der Klügste und Weiseste über sein Zeitalter hinausdenken? Vielleicht fünfzig, vielleicht hundert Jahre, wenn er ein Seher oder ein Genie ist.

Müsste dieses Bewusstsein nicht die Kraft der Aufwärtswollenden lähmen? Nein. Die rastlose Bewegung nach oben ist ja ein Instinkt, ein sonnenhafter, eine zwingende Naturnotwendigkeit ist er, ein Gemusstes, wie der Baum in jedem Jahr einen neuen Ring ansetzen muss. Es steht gar nicht in unserer Macht, uns nicht zu veredeln, zu vervollkommnen.

I feel like someone who is mute and wants nothing more than to speak but can't, just can't.

And no one helps me, no one. I am alone.

The enlightened, they have had years of training and travelling, they have studied countries and people, they have read entire libraries, they have hung onto the every word of wise teachers. Those who wish to reach the top must climb, step by step, and they must have a guide. Wanting to fly without wings: absurdity! megalomania!

Or not so absurd after all? Could one disregard everything which has been previously thought and, surpassing each generation of pioneering minds, generate creative thoughts from the primal source of one's own soul? I have tried it. I have pondered and pondered over the purpose of our being and found nothing but the platitude that every human has no other purpose, can have no other purpose, than that of the stone, the plant, the earth: to be, to grow, to die.

Clearly, the plant is worth more than the stone, the animal more than the plant, the human more than the animal, but not much more, not much.

And if I could recognize and discover what the best of all time recognized and discovered, it would not be enough for me, not enough.

How far beyond their age can even the cleverest and wisest think? Perhaps fifty, perhaps one hundred years, if they are a prophet or a genius.

Shouldn't this awareness paralyse the will of those who desire progress? No. Indeed, restless movement upwards is an instinct; sun-like, compelling, it is a natural necessity, a 'must', like how the tree *must* grow a new ring every year. It is not within our power *not* to improve, to try to perfect ourselves.

Und dieser Instinkt der Veredlung, der ist es, der mich forttreibt, und ich muss ihm folgen, ja, ich *muss*.

* * *

And this instinct for improvement, that is what drives me forwards, and I must follow it, yes, I *must*.

Acht Tage *später.*

Am Meer! Nordsee! Starker nordischer Wind umbraust mich. Er erfrischt mir Leib und Seele.

Immer nur wandle ich am Strand entlang, weiter und weiter.

Eine Düne springt vor, ich will wissen, was dahinter liegt – wieder das Meer.

Eine neue Krümmung – weiter – weiter! immer das Meer, dasselbe, dasselbe.

Nein, doch nicht dasselbe. In der Frühe noch umschmeichelten kosend die Wellen das Land, und gegen Abend, da packen sie es mit Riesenkrallen, heulend, würgend, als wollten sie es zerfleischend, in ihrem finsteren Schoß begraben,

Das rasende Arbeiten der ungeheuren Wassermassen, was schafft es? Nichts. Nachher Alles wie vorher. Und unser Rasen? dasselbe. Nachher Alles wie vorher. Und das Meer rast doch, und wir rasen doch.

Mein Kopf wird frei, die Brust weit in der herb kräftigen Luft. Ist denn das ausgemacht, dass ich alt bin? eine Greisin? Ich bin vielleicht eine Ausnahme der Natur. So wenig Dinge sind bewiesen. Dass gerade das bewiesen ist, dass wir alt werden und sterben müssen! Aber man kann ja hundert Jahre alt werden! Und ich bin erst fünfundfünfzig. Ich habe ja noch beinahe ein halbes Jahrhundert vor mir.

Auf! Frisch! Hinaus! Wandere!

Und ich wanderte frohgemut wohl eine Stunde lang. Vor mir her ging ein junges Mädchen in rotem Kleide. Dann wurde mein Atem kürzer, meine Kraft erlahmte, ich schleppte mich nur so hin, und in bitterer Ernüchterung folgten meine Blicke dem jungen Mädchen in Rot, bis sie sich in der Ferne – ach in so weiter Ferne – verlor.

Eight days *later.*

The sea! The North Sea! A strong, Northern wind roars around me. It refreshes my body and soul.

I do nothing but wander along the beach, further and further.

A dune juts out, and I want to know what lies behind it – the sea again.

Another crook – further – further! still the sea, the same, the same.

No, but not the same. Early in the morning, the sweet-talking waves were still caressing the land, and towards the evening, they seized it with giant claws, howling, retching, as if they wanted to tear it apart, to bury it in their dark bosom.

The relentless raving of the immense masses of water, what does it achieve? Nothing. Afterwards, Everything as before. And our raving? the same. Afterwards, Everything as before. And yet the sea still raves, and yet we still rave.

My head clears, my chest expands in the tangy air. Has it been decreed that I am old? an old woman? Perhaps I am an exception to nature. So few things are proven. But it is indeed proven that we must grow old and die! But one can live to be a hundred years old! And I am only fifty-five. I still have almost half a century ahead of me.

Up! Alive! Out! Wander!

And I wandered cheerfully for about an hour. A young girl in a red dress walked ahead of me. Then my breath became shorter, my strength faltered, I dragged myself along, and, with bitter disillusionment, my eyes followed the young girl in red until I lost her in the distance – oh, so far away.

Nein, ich bin keine Ausnahme, ich werde nicht hundert Jahre alt, ich werde – – nichts werde ich. Ich bin eine angefangene Sache, die nicht fertig wird, nie.

* * *

Am schönsten ist das Meer in den Stunden, die der Nacht vorangehen. Abends, wenn die Flut sich zurückgezogen, dann spiegeln sich die Sonnenreflexe in dem leise verrinnenden Wasser am Strand mit einem süßen, seidenweichen Schimmer von unendlicher Zartheit, bläulich oder rosig. Diese süße Lauheit in der Farbe des Wassers, die schwärmerisch zarte Tönung wirkt wie verhallende Aeolsharfen oder wie der Hauch eines Liebesseufzers auf einer Flöte.

So müsste das Greisenalter verrinnen, eine sanft hinhallende Abendandacht.

Etwas Rührendes haben die Schaumflöckchen, die die Brandung auf den Sand wirft und die nun außerhalb ihres Elements zitternd, frierend zurückbleiben, bis der Sand sie aufsaugt. So ein Meeresschaum bin ich auch, aus meinem Element gerissen, und der Sand saugt mich auf – heut – morgen. – Was ist denn noch von mir übrig? Aber ich bebe noch und friere.

* * *

Heute in lichtloser Dämmerstunde wehte ein kalter Wind. Am Himmel dicht geballte Wolken. Grünlich nächtig das Meer. Öde und nass der Strand. Die weite Farblosigkeit nur von dem weißen Schaum erhellt. Ich fühlte die Kälte bis in's Mark. Und doch stand ich wie gebannt. Und als ich später mein warmes, freundliches Zimmer betrat, kam ich mir wie versprengt vom Weltall vor, es zog mich zurück zu dem lichtlosen Strand, hinaus in das Unabsehbare, das Riesenhafte. Und vor dieser grandiosen Lieblosigkeit, in dieser menschenfernen Weltallsstimmung verlor ich das Gefühl meiner Persönlichkeit und floss fort mit den wallenden Wogen in's Unermessliche hinaus.

No, I'm no exception, I won't live to be a hundred, I won't – – I won't be anything. I am a thing begun that will not be finished, never.

* * *

The sea is most beautiful in the hours that precede the night. In the evening, when the tide has receded, the reflections of the sun are mirrored in the gently ebbing water on the beach with a sweet, silky-soft shimmer of infinite tenderness, bluish or rosy. This sweet luke-warmness in the colour of the water, the rapturously delicate hue has the effect of echoing aeolian harps or the breath of a love sigh on a flute.

This is how old age should fade away, a softly echoing evening prayer.

There is something touching about the little flakes of foam that the surf throws onto the sand and which now remain shivering and freezing outside their element until the sand absorbs them. I am one such sea foam, torn from my element, and the sand drinks me up – today – tomorrow. – What is left of me? But I'm still shivering and freezing.

* * *

A cold wind blew today in the lightless twilight hour. Thick clouds in the sky. The sea a greenish night colour. The beach barren and wet. The vast colourlessness illuminated only by the white foam. I felt the cold to my core. And yet I stood mesmerised. And when I later entered my warm, friendly room, I felt as if I had been scattered from the universe, drawn back to the lightless beach, out into the unforeseeable, the expansive. And in front of this grandiose loveless-ness, in this distant atmosphere, I lost the feeling of my Self and drifted away with the flowing waves into the immeasurable.

Ich habe oft das unheimliche Gefühl, dass ich nicht mehr weiß, ob ich bin und wer ich bin.

Dann spreche ich wohl ein Dutzend Mal den Namen Agnes Schmidt vor mich hin, aus Angst ich könnte ihn vergessen. Aber ich will ihn ja vergessen. Ich und Agnes Schmidt? Was haben wir gemein?

* * *

Ich suche gern eine schmale, von hohen Dünen eingefasste Stelle des Strandes auf, wo nichts ist als das Meer, das graue Meer mit den weißen Schaumkronen. Wenn ein starker Wind weht und der fliegende Sand wie etwas Lebendiges in unheimlicher Eile den Strand entlang huscht, und die graugrünen Gräser auf den Dünen zitternd ineinander fahren, so fühle ich mich eingehüllt von der großen schwermütigen Einsamkeit wie in ein Büßergewand.

Ich bin ja auch eine Büßende. Wessen Schuld büße ich?

Wirr stürzen in mir die Gedanken über- und durcheinander. Ein Chaos, aus dem es blitzt und grollt. Bald taucht ein himmlisches Licht auf, bald sehe ich durch einen Spalt die Hölle gähnen.

Oft, wenn die Flammenstreifen am Himmel sich in dämmernd metallischen Funkeln im Wasser reflektieren, und ich halbschlummernd am Meer liege, dann weiß ich nicht, ob ich träume oder ob ich Visionen habe.

Heut war mir's, als ob ich in der Luft auf einer Strahlenbrücke stünde. Ein Zug von Genien, mit Rosen bekränzt, schwebte mir entgegen, unter süßem Gesang Blumen streuend. Ich strecke die Hand aus nach den Blumen. Da braust aus dunklem Gewölk jäh eine wilde Jagd heran. Eisigen Atem hauchen die Dämonen, und der Atem wird Sturm. Und er übertäubt den Gesang, und Blumen und Genien wirbelt er fort. Und mich auch.

I often have the uncanny feeling that I no longer know *whether* I am or *who* I am.

Then I say the name Agnes Schmidt to myself probably a dozen times for fear I might forget it. But I want to forget it. Me and Agnes Schmidt? What do we have in common?

* * *

What I want to find is a small place on the beach, surrounded by high dunes on all sides, where there is nothing but the sea, the grey sea with its white crests. When a strong wind blows, and the flying sand whips across the beach in an uncanny rush like something living, and the grey-green blades of grass on the dunes thrash, shuddering, into each other, I feel as though shrouded by a great melancholy loneliness, like a penitential robe.

I am a penitent. For what fault am I repenting?

Within me, thoughts tumble wildly over and through one another. A chaos, spitting out thunder and lightning. Now appears a heavenly light, then I see through a fissure the yawning pit of hell.

Often, when the streaks of flame in the sky reflect in the dim metallic sparks of the sea, and I'm lying half asleep by the water, I don't know if I'm dreaming or having visions.

Today I felt as though I were standing in the air on a bridge of light. A procession of wisps, wreathed in roses, floated towards me, scattering flowers while singing sweetly. I'm stretching out my hand for the flowers. Then, suddenly, a hunting party is blustering through the dark clouds. The demons huff out icy breaths, and that breath becomes a storm. And it muffles out the song and whisks the flowers and wisps away. Taking me along with them.

Ich stürze hinab, und ich liege am Strande mit einer Wunde in der Brust. Der Sand trinkt mein Blut, und lange, rötliche Gräser wachsen hervor, scharf wie Schwerter. Und die Dämonen sind Furien geworden und bedrohen mich – Was wollt Ihr – Ihr von mir?

Ein Totes rächen? ein Getötetes? eine Seele? Aber ich bin ja das Opfer! das Opfer bin ich. Unglück ist nicht Schuld.

Der letzte Schimmer der untergegangenen Sonne erlosch. Die Vision entschwand. Geister will ich schauen! Geister! und ich sehe nur Gespenster. Oder bin ich selbst – – ein Gespenst, das Gespenster sieht! Tollkomische Vorstellung!

* * *

Sturm! Sturm auf dem Meer! die entfesselte Wildheit tut mir wohl. Schwarze Wolken jagen über den Horizont. Plötzlich bricht eine furchtsame, blasse Sonne hervor, aber schon jagen neue Wolken hinter ihr her und löschen das zarte Licht. Die paar Bäume am Strand krümmen sich winselnd, wie Lebendiges, das gepeitscht wird. Mehr! Mehr! Ich liebe diese Posaunenklänge der Luft, das heulende Zischen, das schauerliche Aufjauchzen. Riesenseufzer, als wollten sie die Brust der Natur sprengen. In dieser dithyrambischen Wollust ist zugleich höchste Bejahung und Verneinung des Lebens. Wahnsinn und Begeisterung ist im Sturm, etwas das hinaus will aus dem engen Kreis unseres kleinen Planeten. Ja – hinaus! hinauf!

Im Sturm am Meer ist es mir offenbar geworden. Jetzt weiß ich's. Ich weiß es bestimmt, hinaus in alle Winde ruf' ich's: Seelenmord! Wer tat's? Niemand. Alle. Meine Eltern? Mein Mann? Nein. Sie sind unschuldig. Dass ich hundert Jahre zu früh geboren wurde, das ist's. Wenn meine Zeit kommen wird, dann bin ich tot, vermodert, lange schon. Zur rechten Zeit geboren werden und im richtigen Lande, davon hängt alles ab. Dass ich in Berlin geboren wurde, damit fing mein Unglück an. In Süditalien oder in Indien, wo Palmen rauschen und die Sonne ist, die nicht untergeht, da hätte meine Heimat sein müssen.

I plummet down and lie on the beach with a wound in my chest. The sand drinks my blood and tall reddish blades of grass grow forth, sharp as swords. And the demons have become furies and threaten me – What do you want – What do you want from me?

To avenge the dead? the murdered? a soul? But I am the victim! the victim is me. Misfortune isn't a fault.

The last shimmer of the setting sun is extinguished. The vision disappears. I want to see spirits! Spirits! and all I see are ghosts. Or am I myself – – a ghost, that sees ghosts! A funny idea!

* * *

Storm! Storm on the sea! the unrestrained wildness does me good. Black clouds rush over the horizon. Suddenly a nervous, pallid sun breaks through, but new clouds are already chasing after her and snuff out the delicate light. The few trees on the beach crumple over whimpering, like something living that has been lashed. More! More! I love this trumpeting of the air, the howling hissing, the unnerving cheering. Great sighs, as though they wanted to burst Nature's breast. In this dithyrambic voluptuousness is at once the highest affirmation and the negation of life. Madness and elation are in the storm, something that wants to get out of the narrow circle of our little planet. Yes – out! up!

In the storm by the sea, it's become clear to me. Now I know. I know for sure; I shout it to the winds: my soul is dead! Who killed it? No one. Everyone. My parents? My husband? No. All innocent. Being born a hundred years too early, that's it. When my time finally comes, I'll be long gone, dead, decayed. Being born in the right place at the right time, that's what everything is dependent upon. My misfortune began when I was born in Berlin. In the south of Italy or in India, where the palm trees rustle and the sun never sets, that's where my home should have been.

Was hätte aus mir werden müssen? Malerin etwa? Ja, durstig, mit Inbrunst hängen meine Augen an dem Antlitz der Natur. Ich verstehe ihre sanfte und ihre wilde Sprache. Aber ich kann ja den Pinsel nicht führen.

Oder Schriftstellerin? Ich schaue, ahne, denke. Ich möchte schöpfen, schöpfen aus der Tiefe meiner Brust, da rinnt ein Quell, aber ich habe kein Gefäß zum Schöpfen und die lebendigen Wasser verrinnen, verrinnen, und mein Herzblut mit. Ich kann weinen, bitterlich aber ich kann die Tränen nicht schildern. Was ich empfinde, wild ist's wie das Meer, rauschend, unermesslich, tödlich. Ich kann es nicht sagen. Raphael, sagt Lessing, wäre, auch ohne Hände geboren, der größte Maler geworden. Mag sein. Aber er hätte mit Selbstmord oder Wahnsinn geendet. Ich stoße zuweilen einen lauten Schrei aus, ein "Wehe", als gehörte ich zum Chor einer griechischen Tragödie, aber nur wenn das Meer laut aufbrüllt, so dass Niemand ihn hört, auch ich selbst nicht. Es ist so lächerlich. Ich bin ja nur eine alte Witwe! Das weise Kind!

* * *

In tiefer, tiefer Not bin ich! Zu wem rufe ich? Gebet? Ja, ich möchte das Kreuz umklammern, irgend ein heiliges Symbol. Ach, ich bin nicht geboren, um zu glauben. Der Himmel ist mir zu niedrig, der Glaube zu kinderhaft, zu selbstsüchtig.

Höher, höher hinauf wächst mein maßloses Sehnen, Welten zu, wo kein morscher Leib die flammende Seele einsargt. Immer *müssen*! leben müssen! sterben müssen! so gerade denken müssen! Freiheit will ich! körperlose, schrankenlose!

Warum musste ich leben, wie ich gelebt habt? weil ich ein Weib bin und weil auf uralten erzenen Gesetztafeln geschrieben steht, wie das Weib leben soll? Aber die Schrift ist falsch, falsch ist sie!

Warum hat Niemand die falsche Schrift gelöscht?

What would have become of me? Perhaps I'd be a painter? Yes, with fervent zeal my eyes latch thirstily onto Mother Nature's visage. I understand her mild language, her wild language. But I can't wield the paintbrush.

Maybe a writer? I see, I sense, I think. I want to create something, craft something from the depths of my chest, where a spring flows free; yet there's no vessel for me to draw from and the bubbling waters are trickling away, they trickle away, taking my life blood with them. I can weep, bitterly, yet I can't describe the tears. What I feel, it's wild like the sea, glittering, vast, and deadly. I can't put it into words. According to Lessing, Raphael would have been the greatest painter even if he had been born without hands. Quite possibly. But in the end, he'd have taken his own life or gone mad. Sometimes, I let out a loud cry – woe to me! – as if I belonged to the chorus of a Greek tragedy, but only when the sea is roaring loud enough for it to go unheard, even by me. It's preposterous really. I'm just an old widow! You wise child!

* * *

I am in deep, deep distress! Whom can I turn to? Prayer? Yes, I want to embrace the cross, some holy symbol. Alas, I was not born to have faith. Heaven is too low for me, faith too childish, too self-serving.

Higher and higher still, my boundless longing rises towards worlds where no decaying body can bury the flaming soul. *Must* always! must live! must die! must think this way! Freedom is what I want! disembodied, unrestrained!

Why did I have to live as I have? because I am a woman and because it is written on the age-old Tablets of Stone how a woman should live? But the scripture lies, it lies!

Why has nobody destroyed the lying scripture?

Weil man Buchstaben von Erz nicht löschen kann?

So zerschmettere man die Tafeln, wie Moses auf dem Sinai tat. Man zerschmettere sie!

* * *

Because you can't erase letters from ore?

That's why the Tablets must be shattered, just as Moses did on Mount Sinai. Shattered!

Ich hatte wieder eine Vision.

Ich sah einen langen Zug von Schwänen über das Wasser gleiten. Ihr weißes Gefieder glühte in rosigem Abendlicht. Und die Schwäne sangen ihr Schwanenlied, so todestraurig, so herzzerfließend, dass von ihrem Singen sich's unten auf dem Grund des Meeres rührte. All die zarten, bunten Seesterne und die silberschimmernden Fische sah ich unter der Oberfläche des Wassers durcheinander gleiten, und mitten unter ihnen tauchte ein Kopf auf, der Kopf einer Toten, einer Ertrunkenen.

Grauenhaft. Schilf in dem weißen, triefenden Haar, in den leeren Augenhöhlen phosphoreszierendes Licht.

Und schaudernd sah ich, der Kopf – mein Kopf. Aber nein, das war ja der Kopf, der auf der Bildsäule in dem verwitterten Gärtchen fehlte. Auch mein Kopf? Ich halte ihn, ich halte ihn mit beiden Händen, fest, fest.

Und nun wusste ich es mit einem Mal. Ja, lange schon, lange habe ich Selbstmordgedanken.

Das Meer zieht mich hinab. Der nordische Wind hat meine Nerven zu hoch gespannt, gespannt zum Zerreißen. Fort muss ich, dahin, wo milde Lüfte wehen, wo Sonne ist und der Wind an Palmen rührt.

Italien!

* * *

I had another vision.

I saw a long procession of swans, gliding across the water. Their white plumage glowed in the rosy light of the evening. And the swans sang their swansong, so desperately inconsolable, so heart-wrenching, that their singing stirred the very depths of the sea. I saw all the delicate, colourful starfish and the shimmering silver fish gliding about beneath the surface of the water; and in the midst of it all, a head emerged, the head of someone dead, someone drowned.

Ghastly. Reeds in its white, dripping hair, phosphorescent light in its empty eye sockets.

With a shudder, I looked at the head – my head. No, it was just the missing head from the statue in the overgrown garden. Could it be mine too? I hold it, gripping it tightly, tightly with my hands.

That's when it hit me. Yes, for a long time, a long time now, I've been contemplating suicide.

The sea pulls me down. The Nordic wind has stretched my nerves too tightly, tight enough to rip them to pieces. I must leave, go to where the gentle breezes blow, and the sun shines and the wind caresses the palm trees.

To Italy!

* * *

Acht Tage *später.*

In Florenz. Hier bleibe ich nicht lange. Kein Ort für mich. Blumen und Gesang und Heiterkeit und Grazie.

Ein Land für die Jugend. Abseits stehe ich da. Und doch, wenn ich zu dem herrlichen Platz von San Michele und der Kirche von San Miniato hinaufsteige – ich tue es fast täglich – und von Sonne und Schönheit durchglüht bin, dann kommt mir zuweilen der Gedanke, als könnte ich doch noch in der Welt einen Platz ausfüllen, vielleicht in einem Kloster Kinder erziehen. Bin ich aber eine Stunde später wieder in meinem Zimmer, so ist das Feuer erloschen. Es war ja nur ein Reflex der Sonne von Florenz. Ich falle kraftlos zusammen.

Ich sah ein Mädchen, das aus einem Marmorbassin Wasser schöpfte. Sie trug eine rote Bluse und einen hellen Rock. Von höchster Anmut war es, wie sie, auf den Fußspitzen stehend, den Oberkörper hintenüber geneigt, den hellen Wasserstrahl in einem kupfernen Gefäß auffing. Das schwarze Haar hing ihr wirr über die Stirn. Die dunklen Augen lachten. Blühendes Leben. Blühender Leib. Woran erinnerte mich nur das Mädchen? Ich trat zu ihr heran, unwillkürlich fiel mein Blick auf den Wasserspiegel, und ich sah ihr Bild neben dem meinen. Still schlich ich von dannen.

Ich weiß nicht, wieso ich mit einem Mal an meinen sechzehnten Geburtstag zurückdenken musste. Ich trug an dem Tage ein weißes Kleid und im Haar eine Georgine.

Eduard wollte kommen. Ich war vor den Spiegel getreten, aber nur um die Blume zu befestigen, an mein Aussehen dachte ich nicht. Und nun, nach vierzig Jahren tauchte dieses Spiegelbild aus meinem Gedächtnis auf, ein Gesicht mit strahlenden, dunklen Augen, einer schweren, schwarzen Flechte und blühend rosigen Farben. Ja, jenem Mädchen vom Bassin war ich ähnlich gewesen. Eine bittere Wehmut feuchtete mir die Augen, weil ich nicht gewusst habe, dass ich schön und jung war.

* * *

Eight days *later*.

In Florence. I won't stay here long. No place for me. Flowers and songs and merriment and grace.

A land for the young. I stand apart. And yet, when I climb up to the magnificent San Michele square and the San Miniato church – as I do almost every day – and am glowing with sunshine and beauty, I sometimes feel as if I could take up a place in this world after all, perhaps raise children in a convent. But when I'm back in my room an hour later, the fire has died out. It was nothing but a reflection of the Florence sun. I collapse helplessly.

I saw a girl drawing water from a marble basin. She wore a red blouse and a light skirt. She was the epitome of grace, standing on her tip-toes, her upper body tilted backwards, as she caught the bright stream of water in a copper vessel. Her black hair hung tangled over her forehead. Her dark eyes laughed. Blossoming life. Blossoming flesh. Yet what did the girl remind me of? I stepped towards her, my gaze falling involuntarily onto the mirror of the water, and I saw her image next to mine. I slipped away in silence.

I don't know why I was suddenly compelled to think back to my sixteenth birthday. I wore a white dress that day, and a dahlia in my hair.

Eduard wanted to come. I had stepped in front of the mirror, but only to fix the flower, I wasn't thinking about my appearance. And now, after forty years, this reflection emerges from my memory: a face with radiant dark eyes, a heavy black plait, and blossoming rosy colours. Yes, I had been like that girl by the basin. A bitter nostalgia moistened my eyes, because I had not known that I was beautiful and young.

* * *

Ich wollte gleich wieder fort von Florenz, und nun kann ich mich nicht losreißen. Der herrliche Garten des Palazzo Pitti, der Boboli-Garten hat es mir angetan.

Und dieser Palast, Jahrhunderte steht er wie ein Fels in der Brandung der Zeit, und seit Jahrhunderten rauscht der Wind durch seine immergrünen Eichen.

Stein und Baum, ich beneide sie.

Sein! Sein! nur nicht Nichtsein!

Dass ich so viel Wesens um mich mache! Was liegt an dem Einzelnen!

Aber die Gattung vergeht doch so gut wie der Einzelne es dauert nur etwas länger. Die Erde wird erkalten, und nie mehr werden Menschen auf ihr wandeln. Welcher Zeitraum ist der Rede wert, wenn man ihn an Ewigkeiten misst!

So habe ich Recht, um mich zu weinen, dass ich nun zu spät erwacht bin, da es zur Neige geht. Das Unrecht, das man mir getan, man hat es Allen getan. Was in mir erlöst sein will, zugleich will es Andere erlösen. Hindert Ihr den Baum am Wachstum, Ihr tötet auch die Früchte, Ihr tötet die Schatten, die Andere erquickt hätten.

Oft zähle ich in rasender Angst die Minuten. Wie wenige bleiben mir noch! Dann stirbt Agnes Schmidt. Aber ich? ich auch?

* * *

I wanted to leave Florence immediately, and now I cannot tear my-self away. The marvellous garden of the Palazzo Pitti, the Boboli Gardens, did this to me.

And this palace, for centuries it has stood like a rock against the surf of time, and for centuries the wind has rushed through its evergreen oaks.

I envy them, the rocks and the trees.

To be! To be! just not *not* to be!

So much concern about myself! As if the individual were significant!

But the species dies away as well as the individual, it just takes a little longer. The Earth will go cold, and never again will mankind walk over her. What length of time is worth talking about when it is meas-ured in eternities?

So I have a right to weep for my Self that I have awakened too late, now that it is coming to an end. The injustice done to me has been done to all. What wants to be redeemed in me wants to redeem oth-ers as well. If you prevent the tree from growing, you kill the shade that would have provided refuge for others.

I often count the minutes in frenzied fear. How few I have left! Then Agnes Schmidt dies. But me? Me too?

* * *

Ein vegetierendes Naturdasein ohne Intelligenz, ob das nicht wirklich das beste Glück ist? Ein Bursche ist in dem Hause, wo ich wohne, kaum achtzehn Jahre alt. Er sitzt so den ganzen Tag draußen auf den Stufen der Treppe und singt, singt wie ein Vogel in den Zweigen, immer dasselbe, dieselbe Melodie, bald in trauriger, bald in lustiger Weise. Ich sehe ihn nie betrübt oder verstimmt, immer nur mit dem Ausdruck glücklicher Heiterkeit. Und der Grund? Ein paar Gran weniger Gehirn als andere Menschen.

Ist nicht in der Tat der Wahnsinn viel mehr ein Stück lauterer Natur als unser abgerichteter Verstand? Der Wahnsinn läßt Eindrücke und Vorstellungen auf sich wirken, wie die Sonne auf die Pflanze wirkt, wie der Sturm auf das Meer, ohne Kritik, ohne Abwehr.

* * *

A vegetating natural existence without intelligence, isn't that really the greatest happiness? There is a boy in the house where I live who is barely eighteen years old. He sits outside all day on the steps and sings, sings like a bird in the branches, always the same thing, the same melody, sometimes mournful, sometimes cheerful. I never see him sad or out of tune, always with an expression of blissful happiness. And the reason? A little less brain matter than other people.

In fact, is madness not much more a piece of pure nature than our trained mind? Madness is affected by impressions and ideas like the plants are affected by the sun, like the sea by the storm, without criticism, without defence.

* * *

Ich bin gern auf Kirchhöfen. Unsere Gedanken ähneln da den Gedanken, die wir haben, wenn wir krank sind. Alles Richtige schwindet. Wir werden hellsichtig. Ich liebe es, auf das zu horchen, was die Toten reden.

Auf dem Kirchhof von San Miniato aber, da bleiben sie stumm unter ihren hässlichen Gräbern, Gräbern, die an Rumpelkammern erinnern.

Kleine, rohe Gitter mit Metallringen für Blumentöpfe schließen die Grabstätten ein. In den Blumentöpfen dürftige, verstaubte künstliche Blumen, schwarze oder weiße. An den Gittern hängen Kränze, oder sie liegen auf den Gräbern, Kränze von hässlichen Perlen oder Strohblumen. Kleine, törichte Sächelchen stehen umher, Väschen, Laternen, allerhand kindischer Trödel. Und all das angesichts der herrlichen Apenninenkette, unter dem weiten Horizont, der Abend für Abend in purpurnem Violett eine feierliche Glorie niederstrahlt, angesichts der edel schönen Kirche mit den dunklen Zypressen.

Wie einfach und natürlich wäre es, nur ein grüner Hügel, auf den die Sonne von Florenz scheint. Auf den Hügel, ja. Aber nicht bis zu den Toten käme sie.

Wir suchen doch im Leben immer die Höhe. Und nun – da unten – so tief unten. Kommt Gott zu uns *herab?* wir müssen doch zu ihm *hinauf!*

Ich will nicht begraben sein. Verbrannt. In Flammen!

Sie werden mich ja doch nicht verbrennen. Ich will auf meinem Grabe keine Blumen, keinen Stein, keinen Baum – nichts. Es ist so eine kindisch abergläubische Regung, als würden die Gestorbenen wissen, dass man die Blumen auf ihrem Hügel verwelken lässt, dass man ihnen am Sterbetag keinen Kranz bringt. Wir meinen, dass wir noch nicht völlig tot sind, so lange noch ein Lebender unserer denkt.

* * *

I like being in churchyards. Our thoughts there resemble the thoughts we have when we are ill. Everything trivial disappears. We become clairvoyant. I love listening to what the dead are saying.

But in the churchyard of San Miniato, they remain silent under their ugly graves, graves reminiscent of rubbish dumps.

Small crude grids with metal rings for flowerpots enclose the graves. In the flowerpots are scanty, dusty, artificial flowers, black or white. Wreaths hang from the grids or lie on the graves, wreaths of ugly pearls or straw flowers. Small, foolish trinkets lie around, little vases, lanterns, all kinds of childish junk. And all this against the noble Apennine Mountains, under the wide horizon, that glows every evening in the joyous crimson-lilac glory, and in front of the nobly beautiful church with its dark cypresses.

How simple and natural it would be, just a green hill on which the Florence sun shines. On the hill, yes. But it would not reach the dead.

We always seek the heights in our lives. And now – down there – so far below. Does God come *down* to us? We have to go *up* to Him!

I don't want to be buried. Burnt, in flames!

They won't burn me. I want no flowers, no stone, no tree on my grave – nothing. It is such a childishly superstitious impulse, as if the deceased knew that the flowers on their mound are left to wither, that no wreath is brought to them on the day of their death. We believe that we are not yet completely dead as long as a living person still remembers us.

⋆ ⋆ ⋆

Der Boboli-Garten – vielleicht der schönste Garten der Erde – ist ganz aus grünen Mauern gebildet. Lorbeerbäume, Zypressen, immergrüne Eichen. Auf einem hügeligen Terrain steht er. Man steigt darin auf und ab. Weltabgeschieden wandelt man zwischen diesen luftigen, Wohlgeruch ausströmenden Mauern, den tiefblauen Himmel über sich. Hier und da münden sie auf einen freien Platz, von dem man hinübersieht in die Berge, hinab in das Häusermeer der Stadt. Im Schoß der Berge Dörfer und Städte; einzelne Gehöfte bis hoch in die Berge hinauf. Im Abendlicht erglänzen sie wie funkelnde Edelsteine auf flammendem Schleier.

Das Atmen hier ist eine Lust. Der Herbstduft der Bäume vermischt sich mit dem frischen Atem, der vom Gebirge kommt.

Eigenartig in dem Garten ist auch das Ineinander von Kunst und Natur. Überall Bildwerke, meist von Marmor, einige von Sandstein.

Sie stehen in Nischen und auf freien Plätzen, sie tauchen empor aus Wasserspiegeln, sie winken und locken aus grünen Verstecken, sie heben sich frei vom Äther der Luft ab.

Von einem der Plateaus abwärts zu einem Wasserspiegel, aus dem die Göttergestalt des Neptun ragt, führt eine breite, stolze Allee hochragender immergrüner Bäume. Die Bäume stehen da wie Pfeiler. Bildsäulen lehnen daran, Götter und Göttinnen, freudig und bewegt, in lieblicher Erhabenheit. Eine Allee, als führe sie zum Parnass oder zu einem Gefilde der Seligen.

Gegen den Ausgang dieser Götterstraße zweigen sich von beiden Seiten Alleen ab, wie ich ähnliche nie gesehen; breite, aber niedrige grüne Bogengänge, die Wipfel der immergrünen Eichen engverschlungen, so dicht, dass nur golden dämmernd die Sonnenstrahlen hineinhuschen. Das grüne Dach eine Wölbung von reinster architektonischer Form, die Stämme, die es tragen, phantastische Säulen. Tempelhallen, Loggien Gottes.

The Boboli Gardens – perhaps the most beautiful gardens on earth – are made entirely of green walls. Laurel trees, cypresses, evergreen oaks. It stands on hilly terrain which you have to climb through. Cut off from the rest of the world, you walk through the airy walls which pour with sweet aromas, the deep blue sky above your head. Every now and then, they branch off into an open space, where you can look out onto the mountains and down to the sea of houses in the city. Nestled amongst the mountains lie villages and towns; farms dotted about on the tops of the peaks. In the evening light, they shine like sparkling gemstones on a blazing shroud.

Here, it is a delight to breathe. The autumnal scent of the trees blends with the fresh air wafting down from the mountains.

What's also unique about the garden is how Art and Nature are so intertwined. There are sculptures everywhere, mostly made from marble, some from sandstone.

They can be found in crevices and open spaces, breaking through bodies of water, beckoning and calling from leafy hiding places, rising up from the airy ether.

A bright, proud avenue of towering evergreen trees leads from one of the plains and down to a pool of water, from which a statue of Neptune emerges. The trees stand there like pillars. Statues lean against them, gods and goddesses, joyful and animated, in charming majesty. As if the avenue led to Parnassus, or some other blissful realm.

As this stretch of Gods tails off, the avenue splits off into two, unlike anything I had ever seen before. Green archways, broad but low, the tops of the green oak trees tightly interwoven, so dense that only fading rays of the golden sun can slip through. The green canopy, an arch of the purest architectural form; the trunks which support it, fantastical pillars. Halls of a temple, dwellings of Gods.

An dem einen Ende dieser Tempelhallen ruht in einem Siegeswagen eine marmorne Göttin. Ihr schimmernd weißer Leib lockt. Ich ging, wohin sie lockte, und kam zu einer der schönsten Stelle des Parkes, zu einer ziemlich steil abfallenden Allee.

Da sitze ich nun träumend oft stundenlang, von Lorbeerwänden eingeschlossen. Am Fuß der Allee ein Rasenplatz mit einem Rest alten Gemäuers. Jenseits des Rasens erhebt sich das Terrain wieder sanft mit Gruppen von Laubbäumen im Herbstschmuck, von sinnverwirrender Schönheit.

Das dunkle, herbe Grün der Eichen und Lorbeerbäume erscheint nur als Folie dieser traumhaften, unaussprechlichen Farbenzärtlichkeit. Lauterste Goldtöne, die in's Grünliche, Gelbliche und Rötliche bis in's flammende Rot spielen und allmählich sanft ineinanderfließen. Ein Farbenbild, das aus Licht, Liebe, Duft und Traum gewoben scheint, ein Bild von zartester und bezauberndster Genialität, von kosendem, sphärenhaftem Liebreiz. Ein Regenbogen, der sich einmal darüber spannte, erschien hart daneben. Lautlose Stille. Nur ab und zu ein leiser Windhauch, als käme er aus geheimnisvoller Höhe und brächte selige Botschaft. Selbst das Läuten der Glocken von unten erscheint zu profan für den olympischen Charakter des Gartens.

Ich hörte einmal, wie Jemand im Park sagte: "Nichts als Bäume, das ist doch kein Garten, das ist ein verschnittener, missglückter Wald. Wo bleiben die Blumen?"

Das ist wahr, der Boboli-Garten hat keine Blumen. Und das ist seine Eigentümlichkeit. Nur Baum und Stein. Er braucht auch keine Blumen, er darf keine Blumen haben. Sie gehören nicht hinein. Blumen sind ein Bild der Vergänglichkeit, sie welken über Nacht, wie die Menschen auch. Darum passen auch Menschen nicht in diesen Garten, der etwas Unvergängliches hat, wie für die Ewigkeit geschaffen. Vor Jahrhunderten war er gerade wie jetzt, und nach hundert Jahren wird er noch immer so sein: ernst, groß, klassisch, einsam.

***

At one end of this temple hall, a marble goddess rests in her chariot of victory. Her shimmering white body beckons you closer. Following her beckoning call, I reached one of the most beautiful areas of the garden, an avenue which sloped rather steeply downwards.

Now, I often sit there for hours, dreaming, enshrouded by laurel trees. At the end of the avenue, there's a patch of grass and the remains of an old building. A little further, the land rises up again gently into a group of deciduous trees, bewilderingly beautiful in their autumnal splendour.

The dark, bitter green of the oak trees and laurels seems like a foil to this abundance of indescribable colour, dreamlike and delicate. The boldest hues of gold, which morph into greens, yellows, and pinks, until they become a fiery red, gradually blend into one another. A picture of colour which seems to be woven from light, love, air, and dreams; a picture of the sweetest and most enchanting geniality, of gentle, rounded charm. A rainbow which once stretched over it seems garish beside it now. Silent stillness. Only now and then, a quiet breath of wind, as if it came from some mysterious height, bringing a blessed message. Even the chiming of the bells from down below seems too profane for the Olympian character of the garden.

I once heard someone in the park saying, 'Nothing but trees! That's no garden, that's a just a pathetic attempt at a forest. Where are the flowers?'

It is true, the Boboli Garden has no flowers. And that is its peculiarity. Just trees and stones. It does not need flowers either, it cannot have flowers. They don't belong there. Flowers are an image of transience, they wither overnight, just as people do. For this reason, mankind also doesn't fit into the garden, which has something imperishable about it, as if it was created for eternity. Centuries ago, it was already how it is now, and after a hundred years it will still be so: serious, grand, timeless, solitary.

* * *

Heute schreibe ich im Garten selbst. Die Rosenglut des Himmels zittert auf dem Wasserspiegel des Teiches, und Neptun und all' die andern Göttergestalten blühen aus dem rosigen Äther hervor. Hier begreife ich, dass die Schönheit an und für sich ein Gegenstand der Anbetung sein kann, und dass jene Barbaren, die zur Sonne beteten, Recht hatten.

Unter Zypressen klagen wir anders, als unter blühenden Linden. Keine Seufzer. Kein Schrei wie am Meer. Die dunkle Zypresse weist zum Himmel. Der Schmerz wird weihevolle Traurigkeit, er wird Gebet. Ein stilles Sichverlieren wie ein Glockenton in die Luft.

In einem der kleinen Häuschen auf dem Wege von San Michele will ich wohnen, für immer. Da will ich eingehen zum Frieden.

Ich habe eine lange Weile stillgesessen.

Vor der geklärten Schönheit hier erfasst mich ein Staunen, ein schwermütiges Staunen darüber, dass die Menschen meinen, sie wären das Vornehmste alles Geschaffenen.

Wie? im Weltall ist ein winzig kleiner Stern, die Erde, eine Almosenempfängerin. Ihr Licht und ihre Wärme empfängt sie von andern Planeten. Und auf diesem Stern ein mikroskopisch kleines Wesen: der Mensch.

Und in der Unermesslichkeit des Universums mit seinen unzählbaren Sonnen und Planeten gerade dieses Geschöpfchen dasjenige, wohin alles Übrige zielt? Dies die Krone der Schöpfung?

Unwahrscheinlich.

Verschwände die Erde und mit ihr der Mensch aus dem Weltkreis, vielleicht würde das All nicht tiefer davon berührt, als die Erde etwa von einem Erdbeben auf Sizilien.

Erlischt aber die Sonne, so stürzen tote Sterne in ewige Nacht.

Today, I'm writing in the garden itself. The rosy glow of the sky trembles on the surface of the pond, and Neptune and all the other figures of the gods spring forth from the rosy ether. Here, I realise that beauty can be an object of worship in and of itself, and that those pagans who prayed to the sun had been right.

Under cypresses, we lament differently than under blossoming lime-trees. No sighs. No cries like there are by the sea. The dark cypress points towards the heavens. Pain becomes solemn sadness, becomes prayer. A silent loss of self like a chime in thin air.

I want to live in one of the little houses on the road to San Michele, forever. There, I want to enter into peace.

I have been sitting still for a long while.

Here, surrounded by illuminated beauty, I am seized with astonishment, a melancholy astonishment at the fact that mankind believes itself to be the most distinguished work of creation.

How? In space, a tiny little star, the Earth, receives alms. She takes her light and warmth from other planets. And on this star, a microscopic being: the human.

And in the immensity of the universe with its innumerable suns and planets, is this little creature really the one around which everything else revolves? This, the crown of creation?

Unlikely.

If both the Earth and mankind disappeared from the world, perhaps the universe would be no more deeply affected than the Earth would be by an earthquake in Sicily.

When the sun goes out, though, dead stars will fall into an eternal night.

Und wir hilflose Kreaturen, mit Augen, die weinen, mit Herzen, die brechen, mit Krankheit und Qual, wir, die wir einst nicht waren, und einst nicht sein werden, wir – das Höchste?

Ich kann's nicht glauben.

Welten muss es geben, wo keine Augen weinen, keine Herzen brechen. Wesen muss es geben ohne Jammer und Not, Wesen, die nicht Staub sind, und die in sonniger Seligkeit ewig sind. Eine Seligkeit, wie wir sie in ekstatischen Momenten mit schauderndem Entzücken vorahnen.

Was grüble ich nur darüber? Die Sterne sind so fern, so fern.

Doch auf der Erde ist der Mensch der Gipfel der Schöpfung.

Wirklich? ist er es?

Er ist mehr als all das Tausendschöne, das Wunderholde um mich her?

Die Farbenglorie da oben, ist sie nicht ein Gedicht, groß und schön, wie kein Dichter es dichten kann?

Was wir fühlen, und wäre es jauchzende Lust, ist sie jauchzender als hier all das Strahlen und Blühen und Duften?

Während ich so dachte, fing ein Vögelchen an zu singen. Ich weiß nicht, was für ein Vogel es war. Aber die Töne durchdrangen mich und rissen mir das Herz empor. Und der Vogel, glaubt man, hat, wenn er singt, nicht Gefühl und nicht Intelligenz. Seine Kehle nur ein Instrument. Wer spielt es? Gott? wer ist Gott?

And we helpless creatures, with eyes that weep, with hearts that break, with illness and agony, we that once were not, and one day will not be, we – the pinnacle?

I cannot believe it.

There must be worlds in which no eyes weep, no hearts break. There must be beings without misery and distress, beings who are not dust, and who are eternal in sunny bliss. A bliss which we anticipate in ecstatic moments, with shuddering delight.

What am I brooding about? The stars are so far away, so far away.

But on Earth, man is the pinnacle of creation.

Really? Is he?

Is he more than all the thousands of beautiful, marvellous things around me?

The glory of colour up there, is it not a poem, great and beautiful, such as no poet can compose?

What we feel, and if it were exultant pleasure, is it more exultant than all the radiance and bloom and fragrance?

While I was thinking like this, a little bird began to sing. I don't know what kind of bird it was. But the sound pierced me and tore my heart to pieces. And the bird, it is believed, has no feeling or intelligence when it sings. Its throat is just an instrument. Who plays it? God? Who is God?

Die Schwingungen des Äthers, das Rauschen der Bäume, des Meeres, das Flüstern der Gräser, die Donner der Luft nur ein mechanisches In- und Aneinanderklingen? nicht doch vielleicht eine Sprache, eine beseelte? und wir verständen sie nur nicht? ist sie nicht mit der Musik verwandt? auch die ist wortlos und kann doch so tödlich süß sein, so hinreißend beredt, und sie kann uns erschüttern bis zur Vernichtung.

Die menschliche Kreatur ist von allen Naturgebilden am lieblosesten organisiert. Selbst das erhabenste Denken hängt von einem paar Gehirnfasern ab. Ein Faserchen reißt. Der Denker ist ein Idiot.

Zerreißen aber wilde Erschütterungen das Herz der Erde, durchrasen Orkane die Lüfte, die Natur bleibt dieselbe. Sie heilt die Wunden, die sie schlägt, und blüht fort und fort, unzerstörbar! unzerstörbar!

Aber im Hirn des Menschen entspringen die großen, weltbewegenden Ideen?

Tun sie das?

Oder empfängt sie etwa nur das Hirn in geheimnisvoller Befruchtung? und das Zeugende – nicht vielleicht mit Übersinn geschwängerte Ätherwellen, Geisterflüsterungen, jenseitige Botschaften? – Von wem? von Gott? Wer ist Gott?

Ohnmächtig sind wir. Sterne reißen sich los, immense Welten, und schweifen als Kometen durch das All. Feuer bricht aus dem Schoß der Berge, Wasser aus dem Urgrund der Erde. Berge türmen sich auf Berge. Urkräfte! Riesenkräfte!

Und ich, ich ließ mich festhalten von Fesseln, dünn wie Spinnweben, in der Vorstellung, dass sie unzerreißbar wären. Eine Gefangene – in einer Berliner – Hinterstube. Ich musste lachen bei dieser Vorstellung! laut auflachen!

The vibrations of the ether, the rustling of the trees, the raving of the sea, the whispering of the grass, the thunder of the air just a mechanical in-and-out sound? not perhaps a language, an animated one? and we just don't understand it? Is it not related to music? it too is wordless and yet can be so deadly sweet, so ravishingly eloquent, and it can shake us to the point of destruction.

Of all natural creatures, the human creature is the most carelessly formed. Even the most sublime thinking depends on a few brain fibres. One fibre breaks. The thinker is an idiot.

But if wild tremors tear apart the heart of the Earth, if hurricanes race through the skies, Nature remains the same. She heals the wounds it inflicts and continues to flourish, indestructible! indestructible!

But can great, earth-shattering ideas spring from the human brain?

Can they?

Or is it only the brain that receives them through inscrutable fertilisations? and that which begets – not perhaps ether waves impregnated with heightened senses, spirit whisperings, otherworldly messages? – From whom? from God? Who is God?

We are powerless. Stars tear themselves loose, immense worlds, and wander through space as comets. Fire erupts from the womb of the mountains, water from the bedrock of the earth. Mountains pile up on mountains. Elemental forces! Giant forces!

And I, I let myself be held by shackles, thin as cobwebs, believing that they were unbreakable. A prisoner – in a back room in Berlin. I had to laugh at this idea! laugh aloud!

Manchmal bin ich böse, dass ich so nüchtern gesund bin. Nur krankhafte Menschen sind hellsehend, fernsehend. Weil das Gefängnis der Seele, der Leib durchschimmernd geworden? die Fessel loser?

Wäre ich hellsehend!

Wenn ich etwas tief und geheimnisvoll Quellendes in mir fühle, warum werde ich mir dessen nicht klar bewusst, warum kann es nicht an's Licht?

Ich weiß, ich weiß es, es ist etwas in mir, das mehr ist als ich, etwas, das den Zusammenhang mit der Weltseele sucht. Zusammenhang mit dem flimmernd goldenen Duft da oben, Zusammenhang mit den Göttern da im rosigen Äther, Zusammenhang mit – – –

Ach, es ist ja nicht wahr – Lüge, was ich da so vage zusammenphantasiert habe. Ich belüge mich selbst. Ich dränge nur so in's Weite, Große, weil ich mich vor der Enge der vier Sargbretter fürchte. Ich klammere mich an das Universum wie an einen Notanker. Es ist nicht wahr, dass ich mich still verlieren möchte, wie ein Glockenton in die Luft, nicht wahr, dass ich in Florenz bleiben will in einem Häuschen auf dem Weg nach San Michele. Ich kehre nie hierher zurück. Ich will ja weiter – weiter – immer weiter! bis ich – die Weltseele – – – auch eine Phrase? vielleicht. Wir wissen ja nichts! Nur Funken! sie verglimmen – Asche!

* * *

Sometimes I am angry that I am prosaically healthy. Only sickly people are clairvoyant, far-seeing. Because the prison of the soul, the body has become transparent? the shackle looser?

If I were a clairvoyant!

If I feel something deep and mysteriously agonising within me, why don't I become clearly aware of it, why can't it come to light?

I know, I know it, there is something in me that is *more* than me, something that seeks to be bound with the world's soul. Bound with the flickering golden fragrance up there, bound with the gods in the rosy ether, bound with – – –

Oh it just isn't true – all I have so vaguely dreamed up, lies. I am lying to myself. I only rush into the great expanse because I am afraid of how cramped those four coffin boards will be. I'm clinging to the universe like an anchor. It's not true, I don't want to disappear quietly like a bell's tone drifting into the air, I don't want to stay in Florence in a little house on the way to San Michele. I'm never coming back here. I want to go forward – forward – further and further! until I – the world's soul – – – is that also just a platitude? maybe. We just don't know! Only sparks! they shimmer – ashes!

Seit acht Tagen in Capri. Ich atme nur Duft. So voll Güte ist die Natur. Ihre zärtliche Luft liebkost die faltige Wange wie die rosige.

Von wildschöner Poesie diese Trümmer mit der üppig wuchernden Vegetation. Eine entzückend liebliche Arbeit der Natur an dem Morschen, Verfallenen.

Romantische, traumhaft verzauberte Plätze gibt's in Capri, wo nichts die Einsamkeit unterbricht als das leise Wehen des Windes in den blühenden Gesträuchen; so still ist's, dass oft der plötzliche Flug eines Vogels mich erschreckt. Unsagbar, unsagbar das süße Pathos dieser leise tönenden Einsamkeit. Wohin ich mich wende, ich bin allein in einem Urwald wilder Blumen. Kein Stein, aus dem nicht Kräuter oder Blumen sprießen. Und vor mir, neben mir, überall das Meer, das blaue, ein zerfließendes Juwel an der Brust dieser Landschaft von lieblichster Wildheit, von zarter Grandiosität.

In der Ruhe erscheint das Meer schöner als der blassere Himmel. Das sanft Hinfließende des bläulichen Silbers ist von singendem Rhythmus wie die Verse Homers.

Selbst der Sturm ist hier lieblich. Die blauen Wellen mit den silbernen Köpfchen toben nur wie berauschte Nereiden. Ihr klagendes Grollen sind langgezogene Flötentöne. Sagenhaft rauschen sie an den Felsen auf. Nur die Seefalken schießen im Sturm über das tiefe Ultramarin des Wassers wie Verkündiger düster geheimnisvoller Botschaft. Ein Klingen, Sprechen, Klagen über den Wassern, als lägen in seiner Tiefe die Welträtsel.

Und dass man hier frei ist, frei wie der Vogel in der Luft! Kein abgesperrter Weg, keine Bank, kein Wächter, kein Anschlag, keine Warnung für das Publikum. Man schläft Nachts bei offenen Türen. Verbrecher und Diebe gibt's auf dieser seligen Insel nicht. Wildwüchsig Alles, zaubermärchenhaft.

In Capri for eight days now. I'm breathing in pure redolence. So rich in goods is Nature. Her tender breeze caresses the wrinkled cheek just as the rosy one.

These ruins with the lush, flourishing flora, are of an unrestrained, beautiful poetry. A charming, lovely work of Nature among the decrepit, the decaying.

There are such romantic, dreamlike, enchanted places in Capri, where nothing interrupts the seclusion but the gentle wafting of breeze through the blooming thicket; it's so still that often the sudden flight of a bird is enough to startle me. Indescribable, indescribable is the sweet pathos of this quietly sonorous seclusion. Wherever I turn I am alone in a great forest of wildflowers. Not one stone from which herbs or flowers aren't springing. And before me, next to me, all around, the sea, the blue, a deliquescent jewel upon the breast of this landscape of loveliest wildness, of tender magnificence.

In the calm, the sea seems more beautiful than the pale sky. The gentle flowing of the blueish silver is of a singing rhythm like the verses of Homer.

Here, even the storm is sweet. The blue waves with their little silver crowns simply romp like drunken sea nymphs. Their plaintive rumbles are the drawn-out tones of a flute. Marvellously, they wind out onto the rocks. Only seagulls shoot through the storm over the deep ultramarine of the water like harbingers of some dark, secret message. A sound, a speech, a lament over the waters, as though the world's mysteries lay in its depths.

And that one is free here, free like a bird in the sky! No blocked off paths, no benches, no groundskeepers, no signs, no warnings to the public. At night one sleeps with the doors open. There are no criminals or thieves on this sacred island. Everything growing freely, magically, like a fairytale.

Neptun selbst scheint auf seinen Götterarmen diese Insel aus der Tiefe emporgetragen zu haben.

Ist es Göttliches auch, das meine Seele hier emporträgt?

Einmal, als ich noch klein war, sah ich in einem Berliner Schaufenster eine südliche Landschaft mit verwitterten Säulen, mit Zypressen und Palmen, und seitdem, wenn ich in die Stadt ging, machte ich immer einen Umweg, um zu dem Bilde zu kommen. So unwiderstehlich lockte es mich.

Ist das nicht unerklärlich? Oder erklärt es sich so, dass – –

Es kommt vor, dass Menschen, die ganz jung in fremde Länder ausgewandert sind, allmählich ihre Muttersprache vergessen. Und nach einem halben Jahrhundert vielleicht, wenn sie im Fieber oder im Sterben sind, finden sie sie wieder, die Sprache ihrer Heimat.

Bin ich auch im Fieber oder im Sterben, und finde ich sie hier wieder, meine Heimat? War ich nur verschlagen nach Berlin in die Philipp- und in die Steglitzerstraße? Was sollte ich denn da? Agnes Schmidt! ja – aber ich?

* * *

It seems as though Neptune himself raised this island out of the depths, with his godly arms.

Is it something equally godly that is raising up my soul here?

Once when I was little, in a shop window in Berlin, I saw a Mediterranean landscape, with weathered pillars, with cypresses and palms, and from then on, whenever I went into town, I always made a detour to come back to the picture. So irresistibly did it call to me.

Isn't that inexplicable? or perhaps it explains itself in that – –

People say that those who travel to foreign countries as young children gradually forget their mother tongue. And after fifty years perhaps, when they are feverish or dying, they find it again, the language of their homeland.

Am I also feverish or dying and so will find my home here, once again? Why did I end up Berlin, on Phillippstraße and Steglitzerstraße? What am I supposed to do there? Agnes Schmidt! yes – but what about me?

* * *

Ich gehe auch gern durch die Gassen und Gässchen von Capri. Von fremdartigem Reiz sind sie.

Jedes Häuschen hat seine Veranda und seine Pergola, die säulengeschmückte, und um die Säulen hängt die Rebe, die sich gar lieblich von der weißlichen Mauer abhebt. Wunderlich verzauberte Treppen. Sie führen nach oben in die leere Luft, sie führen hinunter in Höhlen, sie kreuzen, sie verschlingen sich, man sieht nicht, woher sie kommen, wohin sie gehen. Märchenhafte Winkel in den schmalen Gassen, ein schwärzliches Stück Mauer, davor ein Zitronenbaum, dahinter das Meer. Und Blumen! Blumen! Blumen in Scherben, Blumen in dunklen Gefäßen. Sie wachsen aus den Mauern in tollem Geschlinge, sie klettern an schimmligem Gestein empor.

Eine Straße aber gibt's, die nur ein langer, schmaler, überwölbter, steinerner Gang ist, so schmal, dass kaum zwei Menschen nebeneinander gehen können. Und dunkel ist's darin und übelriechend. Unrat in allen Ecken. Und auf diese Gänge öffnen sich Zimmer, auch Läden, in denen Esswaren feilgeboten werden. Treppen führen empor auf Veranden oder zu Wohnräumen. Diese Mauergänge haben wie die Tunnels ab und zu Öffnungen, durch die das Meer blaut und köstliche Seebrise dringt. Und in diesen Höhlen leben Menschen, zufriedene, glückliche, lustige Menschen, und sie sehen den ungeheuren Kontrast nicht zwischen ihrer ästhetischen Misere und der poesietrunkenen Pracht da draußen.

Warum wundere ich mich darüber? Ich blieb ja auch zeitlebens in geistiger Misere, und ganz in meine Nähe waren Bibliotheken voller Geistesschätze.

Ein halb verwitterter Balkon in dieser düster steinernen Gasse ist ganz mit Sonnenblumen geschmückt. Zwischen den Blumen sehe ich oft ein rosiges Gesichtchen auf den Steingang hinausspähen.

I also like to walk through the lanes and alleyways of Capri. They have a strange charm to them.

Every little house has its own veranda and canopy decorated with pillars, and around them hangs a vine which stands out quite beautifully from the off-white walls. Wonderful, enchanting staircases. They lead up into the open air, they lead down into caves, they cross and they intertwine, so you can't see where they came from or where they're going. Whimsical corners in narrow alleyways, blackened stretches of wall, a lemon tree in front and the sea behind. And flowers! flowers! flowers in broken China, in dark vases. They grow from the walls in great tangles, traverse the mouldy stone.

But there's one street which is just a long, narrow, vaulted stone passage, so narrow that two people can barely walk down it side by side. And it's dark inside, and fetid. Filth in every corner. And these passages open out onto rooms and shops where food is being sold. Staircases lead to verandas or living quarters. Every now and then, the walls open out like tunnels, through which the blue of the sea and the taste of its breeze enter. And people live in these caves, satisfied, happy, cheerful people, and they are oblivious to the glaring contrast between their aesthetic misery and the poetry-drunk splendour of the outside world.

Why am I amazed by this? I also found myself in spiritual misery my whole life, yet there were libraries full of intellectual treasures all around me.

In this gloomy, stone alleyway, a half-weathered balcony is completely covered in sunflowers. Between the flowers, I often catch glimpses of a little, rosy face as it peeks out from the stone hallway.

In einem offenen Hausflur näht ein blasses Mädchen an einem Kleid für die Jungfrau Maria. Die nackte, bemalte Holzfigur mit dem Kind im Arm steht vor ihr. Und Mutter und Kind tragen Kronen. Das blasse Mädchen aber hustet unaufhörlich. Und nicht die Himmelskönigin und nicht das Jesukind können ihr helfen, und tragen doch Kronen. Aber sie helfen ihr doch in anderer Weise – durch den Glauben. Das kranke Mädchen wird in der freudigen Hoffnung sterben, jenseits zur Rechten der Mutter Gottes zu sitzen, weil sie ihr doch das schöne Kleid genäht hat.

Die Holzfigur in ihrer Nacktheit ist kein Gegenstand für ihre Anbetung. Die Kleider muss sie tragen, die sie selbst ihr genäht. Dann erst ist sie die richtige Himmelskönigin.

An den Kleidern für meinen Himmelskönig habe ich auch genäht und genäht. Und nun suche ich den Gott dazu, suche ihn – –

* * *

In one open passage, a pale girl is sewing a dress for the Virgin Mary. The naked, painted wooden figure, child in its arms, stands in front of her. Both the mother and child are wearing crowns. But the pale girl is coughing, she cannot stop. And neither the Queen of Heaven nor the baby Jesus can help her, and still, they wear their crowns. But they help her in other ways – through faith. The sick girl will die with the hope and peace that, on the other side, she will sit at the right hand of the mother of God, because she has sewn the beautiful dress.

In her nakedness, the wooden figure is no object of devotion. She must wear the clothes which the girl has sewn herself. Only then will she be the true Queen of Heaven.

I too sewed and sewed away at clothes for my King of Heaven. And now I am searching for a God for it, I'm searching for Him – –

* * *

Oft wandle ich zwischen den Ruinen des Tiberius umher. An einer Stelle scheinen die Trümmer ein Garten steinerner Grabhügel, darauf Riesensträuße gelber Blumen. Gelb? nein Gold. Und nur diese *eine* Farbe, sinnverwirrend reizend. Blumen, wie von der Sonne empfangen, im Äther geboren. Und überall, ringsum das Meer.

Weiterhin führt ein schmaler Gang zwischen zwei zerbröckelten, niedrigen Mauern. Der Fußboden uraltes, römisches Mosaik. Auf den niedrigen Mauern eine Überfülle wilder Blumen; sie brennen in rosiger Glut, sie flammen in Purpur, durchsummt und durchflattert von Bienen und Schmetterlingen. Die Blütenkelche auf beiden Seiten der Mauern berühren sich oben und bilden ein Dach von Blumen. Nie haben meine Lungen süßeren Duft geatmet, nie meine Augen Liebreizenderes geschaut. Und hier, hier hat Tiberius seine Opfer in's Meer gestürzt.

Ist der Mensch wirklich so viel mehr als das Tier? Auch Tiberius? Er, das Raubtier, das zerfleischte, und die er zerfleischte waren doch auch nur Lämmer, sie ließen sich ja zerfleischen.

Ein Rieseneidechs, schillernd in smaragdgrünem Glanz, verfolgte einen Schmetterling. Er rettete sich in den Äther hinauf.

Flügel! ja Flügel!

Auch wir werden einst Flügel haben. Ob wirkliche, ob nur mechanisch entwickelte Kräfte gleich Flügeln – wer weiß es!

* * *

I often wander among the ruins of Tiberius[10]. In one area, the remains look like a garden of stone burial mounds, with huge bouquets of yellow flowers on top of them. Yellow? no, gold. And just this *one* colour, bewilderingly lovely. Flowers which look as if they were given by the sun, born in the ether. And everywhere, all around, the sea.

Further on, a narrow passage leads between two crumbled, low walls. An ancient Roman mosaic underfoot. On the low walls, a profusion of wild flowers; they burn with a rosy glow, blazing crimson, suffused with the buzzing and fluttering of bees and butterflies. The calyxes reach from either side of the wall to touch at the top, creating a roof of flowers. Never have my lungs breathed in a sweeter scent, or my eyes beheld something more delightful. And here, *here* is where Tiberius plunged his victims into the sea.

Is man really so much more than an animal? Even Tiberius? He, the predator, tearing apart his prey, and those he preyed upon were mere lambs, they let themselves get mauled.

A giant lizard, shimmering in emerald-green, pursued a butterfly. It escaped, flying up into the ether.

Wings! yes, wings!

We too will have wings one day. Whether they will be real or just forces mechanically devised like wings – who knows!

⋆ ⋆ ⋆

---

[10] Tiberius was Roman Emperor from AD 14 to 37. The negative and mystical associations Agnes attaches to this historical figure have since the nineteenth century been largely discredited.

Menschen, schön und ergreifend wie die Insel, gibt es hier. Ich habe den Mann gesehen, den ich hätte lieben müssen, wenn ich ihm in jungen Jahren begegnet wäre; ein Mensch, den die Natur in einer Feierstunde geschaffen hat. Ich sehe ihn täglich. Als er zum ersten Mal über die Schwelle des Hôtel Pagano trat, war er ganz in weißen Flanell gekleidet und trug eine Passionsblume im Knopfloch. Seine Züge sind mild und edel, seine blauen Augen tief, kristallen klar, man glaubt die Gedanken hindurch schimmern zu sehen. Er sitzt mir gegenüber bei Tisch. Er ist wie ein Psalm. Ich höre Harfenklänge, wenn er spricht. Er ist Arzt.

Es fragte ihn Jemand, warum er immer Passionsblumen im Knopfloch trüge.

"Es blühen ja hier davon so viele," antwortete er lächelnd.

Ich weiß es besser. Er trägt sie, weil, wie man sagt, in ihrem Kelch die Marterwerkzeuge Christi versinnbildlicht sind. Er trägt sie als eine Mahnung, eine Art Ordenskreuz, ein Zeichen, dass er zu einer Gemeinde gehört, die still sich bildet. Tolstoi ist einer ihrer Ordensmeister. Er sagt es selbst, sein Ideal ist nicht das des größten lebenden Philosophen: "der *Übermensch*"; es ist der "*Mitmensch*". Seine Religion ist Nächstenliebe.

Neulich rühmte Jemand die aufopfernde Sorgfalt, mit der er ein krankes Kind auf Capri pflegt. Er wehrte das Lob ab. Seine Nächstenliebe sei nur ein subtiler Egoismus. "Niemand von uns," sagte er, "wäre im Stande zu essen, aus Scham, während ein Hungriger vor ihm stände". Mache denn das einen Unterschied, ob ein Einzelner vor uns, oder Tausende und aber Tausende hinter uns ständen? Nur weil wir sie nicht sehen? Wir wissen es doch.

There are people here who are as beautiful and captivating as the island itself. I saw the man I should have loved had I met him in my younger years; a man created in one of Nature's hours of celebration. I see him every day. When he crossed the threshold of the Hotel Pagano for the first time, he was dressed entirely in white flannel and wore a passionflower in his boutonnière. His features are mild and noble, his blue eyes deep, so crystal clear that his thoughts seem to shimmer through them for all to see. He sits opposite me at the table. He is like a psalm. I hear the melody of a harp when he speaks. He is a doctor.

Someone asks him why he always wears passionflowers in his boutonnière.

'There are so many of them growing here,' he replied with a smile.

I know better. He wears them because the instruments of Christ's passion are said to be symbolized in their calyx. He wears them in remembrance, a kind of order's cross, a sign that he belongs to a community which is developing quietly. Tolstoi is one of the masters of this order. He says it himself: his ideal is not that of the greatest living philosopher, the '*Übermensch*',[11] it is the '*fellow human being*'. His religion is philanthropy.

Recently, someone commended the self-sacrificing care with which he tended to a sick child on Capri. He rejected the praise. His philanthropy was just a subtle egotism. 'None of us', he said, 'would be able to eat, out of shame, when someone hungry stood before them.' Does it make a difference, then, if one person stands before us, or thousands and thousands behind us? Just because we don't see them? We are aware of them all the same.

---

[11] Agnes is referring here to Nietzsche's concept of the 'Übermensch', a superior man, spiritually and biologically. A woman can never hope to be a 'Übermensch', only to give birth to one.

Wie hätte ich ihn geliebt. Aber ich habe ihn ja geliebt, ob im Traume, ob im geheimnisvollen inneren Schauen, ich weiß es nicht. Ich habe ihn geliebt als Kind, wenn ich verzückt in den Mond schaute, ich habe ihn geliebt, wenn die Poesien, die ich in der Schule las, mich durchglühten. Ich habe ihn geliebt, später, wenn bei mechanischer Hausarbeit seltsame Schauer durch meine Nerven rieselten. Es ist eine alte Liebe, so alt, wie ich selber bin. Er war mir vorherbestimmt. Und nun gehören wir verschiedenen Generationen an.

* * *

Oh, how I would have loved him. But I did love him, be it in my dreams, my innermost reflections, I don't know. I loved him as a child, when I gazed enraptured at the moon, I loved him when the poetry I read at school set my heart aflame. I loved him later, when strange shivers rippled through my nerves as I was doing the house-work. It's an old love, as old as I am. He was destined for me. And now we belong to different generations.

* * *

Wenn wir von Tisch aufgestanden sind, eile ich, so schnell ich kann, auf die einsame Höhe meines Lieblingsfelsens. Unter mir, auf dem Abhang Blumen und balsamische Kräuter, von allen Seiten das silberbläuliche Meer, das in der Sonne erglänzt und sich leise an dem Felsen bricht. In der Ferne die Inseln und Halbinseln des Golfs.

Ich nehme den Hut ab, mein graues Haar weht im Winde. Ich stehe aufrecht, die Hände emporgestreckt, und ob ich Verse spreche, ob ich sie nur empfinde, ob ich sie selbst dichte, ob es die Poesien Anderer sind, ich weiß es oft nicht. Ich pflücke ganze Hände voll wilder Blumen, und auf dem Wege lasse ich sie eine nach der anderen fallen. Er macht täglich denselben Weg, er wird über die Blumen schreiten.

Man erzählt, als ein römischer Held und Kaiser Capri betrat, fing eine verdorrte Eiche wieder an zu grünen. So fängt auch, da er sich zeigt, mein Herz wieder an zu grünen und zu blühen. Wieder? nein, es blüht und grünt zum ersten Mal!

Graues Haar, Falten, Runzeln! bin ich das? Nein, nein. Ich bin *in* mir, *in* mir. Ich stecke nur in einer fremden Haut.

Seltsam, dass die Haut unser Schicksal ist.

Wir haben ein glattes Gesicht. Wir lieben einen Menschen. Schön und gut.

Es zeigen sich ein paar Falten in unserem Gesicht. Wir lieben einen Menschen. Bedenklich.

Wir haben viel Falten. Wir lieben einen Menschen. Lächerlich. Verächtlich.

Oder liegt das Sonderbare darin, dass Herz, Geist und Haut nicht gleichmäßig eintrocknen? Sonderbar? nicht vielleicht natürlich? darum weil etwas in uns ist, das nie welkt, nie stirbt, auch im Tode nicht?

When we get up from the table, I hurry as fast as I can to the lonely height of my favourite cliff. Below me, on the slope, flowers and aromatic herbs, the silver-blue sea on all sides, glistening in the sun and breaking softly on the rocks. In the distance, the islands and peninsulas of the Gulf.

I take off my hat, my grey hair blowing in the wind. I stand upright, hands outstretched, and whether I speak verses, whether I only feel them, whether I compose them myself, whether they are the poetry of others, I hardly know. I pick handfuls of wildflowers, and on the way I drop them one by one. He takes the same path every day, he will walk over the flowers.

It is said that when a Roman hero and emperor entered Capri, a withered oak tree began to green and blossom again. And so my heart begins to green and blossom again, whenever he appears. Again? no, it blooms and greens for the first time!

Grey hair, wrinkles, wrinkles! is that me? No, no. *I* am *in* me, *in* me. I'm just in someone else's skin.

Strange that skin is our destiny.

We have a smooth face. We love someone. Beautiful and good.

A few wrinkles appear on our face. We love someone. Worrisome.

We have a lot of wrinkles. We love someone. Ridiculous. Contemptible.

Or is it not more strange that heart, mind and skin do not dry out as one? Strange? not perhaps natural? is it because there is something in us that never withers, never dies, not even in death?

Kann ich dafür, dass Schätze der Liebe in meiner Brust ruhen, die nie gehoben wurden, und nun hat die Sonne, die seligste Schönheit, sie an's Licht gebracht. Eine Flut ist über mein Herz gekommen! Nicht die Liebe für den Einen nur, die Liebe für Alle, für Alles, was so flammend beredt so voll Frühlingskraft mich überwältigt.

Ich bin ja ein neuer Mensch. Ich bin jung. Ich habe noch nicht gelebt. Ich muss ja jung sein.

Ich habe die psychische Kraft mich zu verwandeln. Wie jene Medien, von denen ich gelesen, die, wenn sie den Geist eines Verstorbenen zitieren, in geheimnisvoller Suggestion Stimme und Gesichtsausdruck des Toten annehmen, so habe ich meine gestorbene Jugend zitiert. Sie ist da, und meine Lippen lächeln mit dem Lächeln jungen Glücks, in meinen Augen ist das Licht der Jugend. Ich bin wahr und wahrhaftig achtzehn Jahr alt. Bräutlich ist mir. Nach Capri habe ich meine Hochzeitsreise gemacht, dem seligen Eiland, das ganz ein Festgemach ist für die Hochzeit zweier Seelen.

* * *

Can I help it that treasures of love lie dormant in my breast that have never been unearthed, and now the sun, the most blessed beauty, has brought them to light? A flood has come over my heart! Not just love for the one, but love for All, for everything that overwhelms me with such flaming eloquence and springtime vigour.

I am a new person. I am young. I have not yet lived. I *must* be young.

I have the mental strength to transform myself. Just like those mediums I have read about who, with secretive suggestion, assume the very face and voice of the deceased person whose spirit they summon, I too summon my dead youth. She's there, and on my lips is the smile of youthful happiness, in my eyes, the light of youth. I am eighteen years old, through and through. I am a young bride. I have come to Capri on my honeymoon, the blessed island, the banqueting hall for weddings of two souls.

* * *

Auf meinen einsamen Spaziergängen bin ich in eine Höhle geraten sie heißt Matromania. Wunderbar diese Höhle mit ihren gewaltigen Wölbungen und Steinblöcken. Innen ist sie tempelartig ausgebaut, ein Rest altrömischen Mauerwerks. Einige Stufen sind erkennbar, die zu einer Art Altar führen. Hier soll Tiberius dem Sonnengott einen Knaben geopfert haben. Eine ganz enge Öffnung blickt man hinaus auf das Meer. Herrlich wirkt es von hier.

Und Tiberius sah diesen hinfließenden Strom herzerschütternder Schönheit, und es bändigte ihn nicht, es rührte ihn nicht.

Plötzlich fiel mir ein, wie, wenn hier ein kleiner Stein vom Gewölbe sich loslöste und zermalmte mich, oder er fiele vor die Öffnung, und ich müsste qualvoll verhungern!

Ja, auch die Natur kann böse sein, böse und grausam.

Und vielleicht war es das, was den Tiberius so böse, so teuflisch machte. Täglich sah er die verderbnisschwangeren Feuersäulen des Vesuvs emporlodern. Er sah Jahr für Jahr, wie das süße blaue Meer und die herrliche Erde sich auftaten und in wildere Gier Lebendiges verschlangen. Hinter gleisnerischer Pracht, überall, überall sah er den Tod. Und das machte ihn wahnsinnig. Und er spie seine wollüstig tierische Grausamkeit der Natur wie einen Riesenhohn in's Antlitz. "Ich bin stark wie Du!" Und bei seinen wilden Totentänzen weinte er Tränen von Feuer.

Darum nennt man auch den feurigen Wein hier Tränen des Tiberius.

Es war dämmerig geworden. Düster glühende Reflexe der untergegangenen Sonne fielen in das tiefe Dunkel der Höhle, und färbten die leise herabsickernden Tropfen rot, rot wie Blut. Ein Schauer durchlief mich. Meine Hände wurden eiskalt, und ich hatte die Halluzination, als fiele der Stein wirklich.

When I was out walking on my own, I came across a cave with the name of Matromania. This cave, with its vast arches and boulders of stone, is wonderful. Inside, it's built like a temple, the remnants of ancient Roman architecture. I can make out a few steps which seem to lead to an altar. It's here that Tiberius is said to have sacrificed a young boy to the God of the sun. A very narrow opening leads into the cave itself. Through this opening, you can see the sea. It looks magnificent from here.

And Tiberius looked at this heart-wrenching beauty as it flowed by, and it neither tamed him nor moved him.

Suddenly, it occurred to me that if one of the small stones were to come loose from the arches, it'd crush me! if it fell in front of the opening, I'd starve an agonising death!

Yes, even Nature can be evil, evil and cruel!

Maybe that's what made Tiberius so evil, so diabolical. Day after day, he saw Vesuvius erupt in pillars of fire, laden with depravity. Year after year, he saw how the sweet blue sea and the glorious earth split open and devoured living creatures with untamed greed. Beyond the façade of splendour, all he saw was death, everywhere. And that drove him mad. So, in an act of mockery, he spat his lustful, animalistic cruelty back in Nature's face. 'I am just as strong as you!' And as he danced his wild dances of death, he cried tears of fire.

That's why they call the fiery wine here the Tears of Tiberius.

Dusk had fallen. Glowing dimly, reflections of the setting sun fell into the deep darkness of the cave, tinging the water droplets red as they trickled softly by, red like blood. A shiver ran through me. My hands were as cold as ice, and I hallucinated that the stones really were falling.

Ich saß da, zitternd, ohne die Kraft, mich zu rühren. Auf dem Altar glaubte ich eine goldene Schale zu sehen, davor ein Greis mit wallendem weißen Bart. Mit einem Stabe berührte er die Schale, eine weißliche Flamme loderte empor, und aus den Flammen entwickelte sich ein Wirrwarr traumartiger Wesen, wild phantastische Fratzen und holde Lichtgestalten in zartfarbigen Schleiern, auf dem wehenden goldenen Haar grüne Kränze. Dann waren es ernste, schöne Frauen, schwarz verhüllt. Und durch all' den bunten Nebel schwirrten feurige Schmetterlinge. Auf den Säulen des Altars saßen Eulen. Halb ein Hexensabbat, halb Feentraum.

Durch den schwarzen Hintergrund der Höhle lief feuriges Zucken, ein jauchzendes Sprühen in allen Farben, blau, rot, grün. Und allmählich entwickelte sich aus dem Sprühen ein Regenbogen, ein strahlender, und er wölbte sich und schwoll, quer durch die Höhle eine Brücke bildend, die in's Freie führte. Und mit einem Male war der Regenbogen eine Schlange, eine glitzernd wunderschöne Riesenschlange, und auf die lebendige Brücke schwangen sich all' die wirren Gestalten und drängten hinaus in's Freie. Und auch ich erklomm die Brücke. Da ringelte sich die Schlange um meinen Leib, und presst mir die Brust zusammen, und die Schlange sprach: "Ich bin ja die Sünde, die Sünde des Tiberius. Ich bin die Brücke, die zur Hölle führt."

Der letzte Sonnenreflex war verglommen. Die Halluzination verschwand. Ich stürzte hinaus aus der Höhle.

Ich meine, man ist verantwortlich für seine Träume und Halluzinationen. Habe ich gefehlt? Womit? Der Mann mit der Passionsblume – ist er es? Ist es, weil ich ihn auch jetzt noch liebe, wenn auch in besonderer Weise? mit einem süßen Frohlocken darüber, dass ich in einem Menschen den Gott gefunden. So lange ich allein bin, weiß ich, dass nichts in mir ist, was das Licht zu scheuen braucht. Sobald ich aber unter Menschen komme, sehe ich mit den Augen der Anderen, denke ich mit den Gedanken der Andern, dann fühle ich mich eines lächerlichen Anachronismus schuldig, und ich schäme mich.

I sat there, shivering, lacking the strength to move. I thought I saw a golden bowl on the altar and, in front of it, an old man with a flowing white beard. As he touched the bowl with his staff, a pale flame began to burn and from it, a confusion of surreal creatures emerged: hideous visages, savage and grotesque, and fair-faced luminaries with pastel-coloured veils, green wreaths in their flowing golden hair. Then there were solemn, beautiful women, shrouded in black. And through this colourful mist came the fluttering of butterfly wings. Owls sat on the pillars of the altar. Half a witches' sabbath, half a fairy dream.

A shudder of flames flared against the black backdrop of the cave, a jubilant spray in all colours, blue, red, green. And, gradually, the spray transformed into a beaming rainbow, and it arched and swelled, forming a bridge across the cave, leading out into the open. And all of a sudden the rainbow was a snake, a glittering, beautiful giant snake, and all of the delirious figures swung onto this living bridge and surged out into the open. And I climbed the bridge too. Then the snake coiled itself around my body, squeezing my chest, and said: 'I am sin, the sin of Tiberius. I am the bridge that leads to hell.'

The last reflection of the sun had died out. The hallucination vanished. I rushed out of the cave.

I reckon we are responsible for our dreams and hallucinations. Have I sinned? What did I do? The man with the passionflower – is it him? Is it because I still love him even now, albeit in a particular way? with the sweet rejoice of having found the divine in a human. As long as I am alone, I know that there is nothing in me which ought to shy away from the light. Yet as soon as I am among other people, I see myself with their eyes, think with their thoughts, then I feel guilty of a ridiculous anachronism, and I am ashamed of myself.

Sinnliche Liebe ist nur wie der Schaum auf einem Getränk. Wenn er verflogen ist, genießt man das Getränk um so reiner. Sinnliches Begehren hat oft mit der eigentlichen geistigen Individualität der Begehrenden nichts zu schaffen, und gemeinsam dabei ist Mann und Weib nur die Erregung des Blutes.

Was für eine dunkle, sonderbare Vorstellung, dass die Liebe zur Erhaltung der menschlichen Gattung da sei, wie die Befriedigung des Hungers zur Erhaltung des Leibes. Die Erregung des Blutes ist wegen der Fortpflanzung da, aber nicht die Liebe, nicht die Liebe.

Ich liebe ihn, nicht wie eine Mutter den Sohn, nicht wie eine Schwester den Bruder, nicht wie die Gattin den Gatten liebt. Freier, reiner ist, was ich empfinde, eine intime, begeisterte Genossenschaft, geboren aus der herztiefen Sehnsucht nach Mehrsein, nach einem Mehrerkennen, Mehrfinden, Weiterschauen. Das zärtliche Ineinanderschmiegen von Stimmungen und Gedanken, ja, auch sie sind eine zarte Wollust, und die Küsse, die nicht auf die Lippen geküsst werden, sondern von Seele zu Seele, auch sie sind eine Ekstase, ein inbrünstiges Erschauern der feinsten Nervendrähte, Funken von der Weltseele abgesprüht.

* * *

Sensual love is just like the foam on top of a drink. When it has evaporated, one enjoys the drink all the more purely. Sensual desire often has nothing to do with unique spiritual identity of the desirer, and for both man and woman it is merely an excitement of the blood.

What a dark, peculiar notion that love is there to sustain the human race, like the satisfaction of hunger sustains the flesh. The excitement of the blood is there for the sake of procreation, but not love, not love.

I love him, not as a mother loves her son, or a sister her brother, or a wife her husband. What I feel is more free, more pure: an intimate, enthusiastic companionship, born of a heartfelt longing to be more, to understand more, to find more, to see further. The intimate caressing of thoughts and feelings, yes, even this is a tender lust, and the kisses, which are not kissed on the lips, but from soul to soul, these too are an ecstasy, a fervent shiver along the finest neurons, sparks sprayed from the world's soul.

★ ★ ★

Was ich da von der Liebe geschrieben habe, ist das nicht öde Phantasterei und völlig unrealistisch? Für Andere vielleicht, nicht für mich.

Die meisten würden das Leben, das ich gelebt habe, durchaus realistisch nennen. Für mich war es nur ein blasses Traumbild. Das Alltagsleben, das sich so mechanisch abspielt, was wir essen, trinken und so daherreden, die physische Liebe, das alles erscheint mir schattenhaft, unwirklich. Unleugbar, unser Körper ist realistisch. Aber nur unser Körper?

Man sagt, der Mensch sei halb Tier, halb Engel. Liegt nur auf der Tierseite das Realistische? Und was wir innerlich leben, was wir in Halbvisionen schauen, was in der Tiefe unserer Brust singt und klingt, mit einem Wort, Alles, was auf der Engelseite liegt, das wäre nicht realistisch? Aber es erfüllt mich, es ist mein Schmerz und meine Lust, meine Verzweiflung und mein Entzücken. Und die Liebe, die ich meine, ist ebenso realistisch wie die Umarmung der Leiber.

Und dennoch – dennoch – Ich bin immer in Angst, man könnte hinter das Geheimnis meiner Jugend und meiner Liebe kommen. Er nicht! er nicht! vor Allem er nicht! Neulich kam er an der Stelle vorbei, wo ich saß. Er grüßte, blieb stehen, er wollte mich ansprechen. Ich gab mir ein verfallenes Aussehen und wandte mich ab. Würde er das Doppelwesen in mir verstehen? Und dass es nicht die alte Frau ist, die ihn liebt, sondern das junge Mädchen, das vor 35 Jahren 18 Jahr alt war?

Nein, ich brauche mich nicht zu schämen, die Anderen müssen sich schämen, weil sie nur das verstehen, was alltäglich geschieht, und was auf der Tierseite liegt, und weil sie nicht begreifen, dass es jedem Alter zukommt, das was liebenswert ist, in's Herz zu schließen.

What I wrote there about love, is it just a dreary fantasy, completely unrealistic? Maybe for others, but not for me.

Most people would call the life I lived quite real. For me, it was nothing more than a pale dream. Everyday life, which happens so mechanically, what we eat, drink and talk about, physical love, it all seems shadowy, unreal to me. Undeniably, our body is real. But only our body?

They say that man is half animal, half angel. Is it only the animal side that is real? And what we live inwardly, what we see in half-visions, what sings and sounds in the depths of our chest – in a word, everything that lies on the angelic side – that would not be real? But it fulfils me, it is my pain and my pleasure, my despair and my delight. And the love I mean is just as real as the embrace of the flesh.

And yet – yet – I am always afraid that someone might find out the secret of my youth and my love. Not him! not him! especially not him! The other day he passed by where I was sitting. He greeted me, stopped, he wanted to speak to me. I gave myself a forlorn expression and turned away. Would he understand the duality within me? And that it's not the old woman who loves him, but the young girl who was 18 years old 35 years ago?

No, I need not be ashamed, the others should be ashamed, because they only understand what happens every day, and what lies on the animal side, and because they do not realise that, at every age, it is possible to welcome something lovable into one's heart.

Auch einer alten Frau? Der siebzigjährige Goethe liebte ein junges Mädchen, um ihrer Jugend und ihres Reizes willen; und Mit- und Nachwelt bewunderte darin Goethe'sche Gemütskraft. Empfindet aber eine alte Frau tief und stark für einen Mann, um seiner Seelen-Schönheit willen, so ist sie – erotisch wahnsinnig.

Arme alte Frau, lass dich nicht, da du noch lebst, in's Totenreich schicken. Ich liebe dich, alte Frau. Ich kenne deine geistigen Mühsale. Ich bin selber alt – – alt? wirklich? oder – –

Ich habe in meinen Kinderjahren eine Geschichte von Jean Paul gelesen von einem alten Menschen, der in einer Neujahrsnacht in marternder Reue über sein vergeudetes Leben verzweifelt. Und da erwacht er. Es war nur ein Traum. Er ist jung. Das Leben liegt vor ihm. Wenn ich nun auch bloß träumte, dass ich alt wäre? Und ich erwachte und wäre jung, und – –

Ach ja! ach ja! Ich habe ja wieder so oft das Gefühl des Schwebens, des Fliegens wie in den Träumen meiner Kinderjahre.

★ ★ ★

Even an old woman? The seventy-year-old Goethe loved a young girl for her youth and her charm; and the world around and after Goethe admired his vigour. But if an old woman feels deeply and strongly for a man for the beauty of his soul, she is – erotically insane.

Poor old woman, do not let yourself be sent to the realm of the dead while you are still alive. I love you, old woman. I know your spiritual labours. I am old myself – – old? really? or – –

When I was a child, I read a story by Jean Paul about an old man who, on a New Year's night, despairs in agonising remorse over his wasted life.[12] And wakes up. It was only a dream. He is young. He has his whole life ahead of him. What if I was dreaming that I am old? And I would wake up and be young, and – –

Oh yes! Oh yes! I have that feeling of floating again, of flying, like in the dreams of my childhood years.

＊ ＊ ＊

---

[12] Agnes is referring to Jean Paul's short story 'Die Neujahrsnacht eines Unglückli-chen' (*The New Years' Eve of an Unhappy Man*). Jean Paul (1763–1825) inspired many German writers in the nineteenth century.

Gestern bin ich wieder zu den Ruinen des Tiberius emporgestiegen. Ich fand Alles in Nebel gehüllt, Himmel und Meer eins. Lichtgrauer, undurchdringlicher Äther, nur ab und zu ein silbriges Glitzern, das gleich wieder verschwand. Die blühenden, farbigen Sträucher unten am Ufer schienen in dem traumhaften Äthermeer zu schwimmen. Säuselndes Tönen über dem Abgrund.

Als allmählich der Nebel wich, erschimmerten die Felsen in mystischem Glanz, in goldigem Grün, dunklem Purpur, welkem Braun. Hier und da ein Sonnenreflex. Schaum spritzte auf. Als ich lange hinuntersah in die quirlenden Wasser, schienen sie Form und Gestalt anzunehmen. Der brandende Schaum wurde zu weißen Leibern, aus den Lichtstrahlen entwickelte sich goldenes Haar. Die Sirenen! Und sie winken und sie locken.

Eine heiße Wehmut machte mich weinen. Zu spät, zu spät begreife ich, wie schön die Welt ist! wie schön!

Nun erglänzt das Meer, nun blüht diese wilde Myrte nur einen kurzen Augenblick für mich, ein Blitz, der in die Finsternis zuckt – dann Nacht.

Weiche, schmerzlichdürstende Melancholie hüllt mich ein, wie die höchste Schönheit sie erregt, die über unser Herz und über unsern Kopf hinauswächst, und die inbrünstig zu umklammern, unser Organismus zu dürftig ist.

Zu schön! zu schön! zu weich und süß und schwelgerisch. Hierher hätte ich nicht kommen sollen. Florenz hatte mir Ruhe und Resignation gegeben, die Nordsee mir Kopf und Nerven gekräftigt. Hier aber ist Alles schmachtend schmeichelnde Liebkosung, nur Blühen und Duften und träumen. Die Insel der Sirenen!

Was war das? Er hat mir einen Myrtenstrauß zugeworfen. Ich sah ihn wohl. Also doch ein Traum, dass ich alt bin? –

Yesterday I climbed up to the ruins of Tiberius again. I found everything swathed in mist, the sky and the sea as one. Light-grey, impenetrable ether, only the occasional argentine gleam that would soon disappear again. The colourful, blooming undergrowth down by the bank seemed as though swimming in the dreamlike sea of ether. Sighing breaths over the abyss.

As the mist gradually retreated, the cliffs shimmered with a mystical lustre, in sweet greens, dark purples, withering browns. Here and there flares of sun. Foam spraying into the air. I gazed down into the swirling water for a while until it seemed to take on form and figure. The surging foam became white bodies, from the beams of light developed golden tresses. Sirens! And they wave and beckon.

A burning melancholy brought me to tears. Only now am I recognising how beautiful the world is, and it's too late, too late! so beautiful!

Now the sea shines, now these wild myrtles bloom, only the blink of an eye for me, only one flash of lightning in the darkness – then night.

A soft melancholy, an excruciating yearning engulf me, provoked by that utmost beauty which blooms out of our hearts and our minds but the organism is too feeble to grasp it fervently.

Too beautiful! Too beautiful! too soft and sweet and bacchanal. I shouldn't have come here. Florence had given me ease and resignation, the North Sea strengthened my mind and nerves. But here everything is a gentle, coaxing caress, only flowers, and fragrance, and dreams. The Isle of Sirens!

What was that? He threw a posy of myrtles to me. I saw him do it. Am I only dreaming that I'm old? –

Ich habe mir aus der Myrte einen Kranz gewunden, und den Kranz habe ich mir auf's Haupt gesetzt. Er war hinter mir fortgegangen. Und doch sah ich ihn, als ginge er vor mir her, und je weiter er sich entfernte, ich sah ihn immer gleich nah.

Ich sah ihn in die kleinen Mauergänge einbiegen, die zum Hotel führen. Eine junge Capresin kam ihm entgegen. Wie schön und anmutig sie war. Er blieb stehen – er – – Ich griff nach dem Myrtenkranz. Er fiel zu Boden. Nun war er mir entschwunden.

Beim Nachhausegehen fürchtete ich mich vor dem Wasserspiegel, vor meinem Bild darin. Ich wollte die Illusion nicht verlieren.

Die Illusion?

Aber er warf mir doch die Myrte in den Schoß!

O du liebster Mensch! Du Bester, du weißt's! Du weißt's!

Erwecke mich! erwecke mich!

* * *

I wound the myrtles into a wreath, and I put the crown on my head. Behind me, he had walked away. And yet I could see him as though he were walking in front of me and as he walked ever further away, he always seemed just as near.

I saw him turn into the little walled walkways that lead to the hotel. A young local girl came towards him. How charming and pretty she was. He stood still – he – – I reached for the myrtle crown. It fell to the floor. Now it was lost to me.

As I returned, I was afraid of the water's surface, of my reflection in it. I didn't want to break the illusion.

The illusion?

But he *did* throw the myrtles into my lap.

Oh, you lovely man! You best of men, you know! You know!

Awaken me! Awaken me!

* * *

Der Geist des Tiberius geht um! Er hat gelogen! sein Antlitz lügt!
Die Passionsblume, die er trägt, ist eine Lüge. Ich habe sie ihm von
der Brust gerissen. Der Duft von Capri, der berauschende, ist Gift.
Das blaue Meer – ja – eine Riesenschlange, eine glitzernde, glei-
ßende! Sirenen! Meine Liebe – Irrsinn! Ich will sie ertränken, ertränken im Meer! tief im Meer, bis sie tot ist – tot. Der Geist des Tiber!

* * *

The ghost of Tiberius is haunting this place. He lied! his appearance lies! The passionflower he wears is a lie! I tore it from his chest. The heady perfume of Capri is poison. The blue sea – a constrictor, a glistening, glittering snake! Sirens! My love – just madness! I want to drown it, drown it in the sea! deep in the sea until its dead, dead. The ghost of the Tiber.

Ich habe es nicht getan. Wozu soviel Lärm machen. Es ist ja so wie so zu Ende. Ruhe! Ruhe, alte Frau!

Ich war ein paar Tage zu zweien. Nun bin ich wieder allein. Einsamkeit – das Leichentuch der Überflüssigen.

Der Mensch im Sarge, der den Deckel hebt, ein wenig hebt, das ist das Bild unseres ganzen Seins. Der Leib – der Sarg. Das brennende Verlangen, hinaus – hinauf! das ist die Kraft, die heben will, will, und nicht kann.

In Capri wäre ich? Nein, in einer Wüste. Meine Lippen brennen, mein Blut brennt – Durst – Durst!

Ich habe von dem Wein getrunken, von den Tränen des Tiberius habe ich getrunken. Ich bin jammerberauscht – berauscht! Nur Ruhe – Ruhe! Fort von hier! Wohin? Gleichviel. Was habe ich ihm getan? Eisige Schauer – eisige Schauer! Und das Hämmern da im Kopf – dumpf, dumpf und stark. Was soll zerspringen!

Das arme Weib! das arme Weib! Miserables Geschlecht. Du hast nicht daran gedacht, eine alte Frau mit Tränen der Begeisterung im Auge – Sappho aus den Fliegenden Blättern. Eine alte Frau, mit einem Herzen, das klopft, mit einem Hirn, das denkt – Großmutter Psyche. Psyche, sagte er, er weiß also, weiß welcher Art ich bin? Und doch – doch –

Auch er! er! so weise, so gütig, so fein! Auch er! Kann er nicht über den Gedankenkreis seines Zeitalters hinaus, wer kann es denn?

Es ist nicht mein Zeitalter, nicht meins! Ich hasse es! hasse es, das elende Zeitalter!

Mein Kopf! mein armer Kopf! am Fuß der Säule, der blutbesprenkelten, liegt er da? oder unter dem Wasser, über das die Schwäne ziehen? Warum haben sie mir das Herz gelassen! das Herz! es muss auch heraus! das zuckende – blutende – –

I didn't do it. Why make such a fuss. It's over either way. Rest! Rest, old woman!

For a few days, there were two of us. Now, I'm alone again. Loneliness – the shroud of the superfluous.

The person in the coffin who lifts the lid, lifts it a little, that's the epitome of our very existence. The body – the coffin. That burning desire, outwards – upwards! That's the strength that wants to lift, wants to, yet can't.

Could I be in Capri? No, a desert. My lips burn, my blood burns – thirst – thirst!

I have drunk wine, the Tears of Tiberius. I'm drunk on misery – drunk! Just rest – rest! Away from here! Where to? no matter. What have I done to him? Icy shudder– icy shudder! And the hammering in my head – dull, dull and powerful. What's meant to burst!

The poor woman! the poor woman! The miserable sex. You've not contemplated an old woman with tears of passion in her eyes – a grotesque Sappho. An old woman, with a heart that beats, a brain that thinks – Grandma Psyche. Psyche, he said, so he knows what kind I am? And yet – yet –

He too! he! so wise, so kind, so fine! He too! If he can't escape his generation's mindset, then who can?

It's not *my* time, not mine! I hate it! hate it, the wretched time!

My head! my poor head! at the foot of a pillar, the one spattered with blood, is it there? or beneath the water, swans gliding over it? Why have I been left with my heart? the heart! that too must be released! the twitching – bleeding – –

Warum musste ich leben wie ich – – schrieb ich das nicht schon einmal – und von den ehernen Gesetzestafeln, die – – und von dem Sarg
– und – man soll sie zerschmett – zermet – mein Gott – wie schreibt
man das Wort? zersch – – wie schreibt man – der Deckel – haltet!
haltet! – er – ich – ja – Asche – –

* * *

Why did I have to live as I – – I've already written that – and about
the Tablets of Stone which – and about the coffin – and – they must
be shatter – sharr – my God – how do you spell it? sha – – how do
you spell – the lid! stop! stop! he – I – yes – ashes – –

Hier endete das Tagebuch. Doktor Behrend fand darin nicht, was er zu finden gehofft hatte: Psychologisches Material für die Entstehung von Geisteskrankheiten. Doch war er von tief menschlicher Rührung ergriffen, als er jetzt an's Bett der Sterbenden trat. Sie saß aufrecht. Ihr Antlitz war schmal wie ein Schatten. Sie trug noch den welken Myrtenkranz. Die spitzen Stängel hatten sich in ihr Haar verwickelt. Man hatte versucht, den Kranz zu entfernen, und sie dabei geritzt. Ein Tropfen Blutes rann ihr über die Stirn. Mechanisch zerpflückte sie die Passionsblume, die auf der Decke lag. Ihre todentzückten Blicke hingen an dem Feuerball der untergehenden Sonne. Als sie jetzt mit einer Stimme, die verhallenden Harfenklängen glich, den Arzt anredete, spielte ein zartes Lächeln um ihre Lippen: "Eine Greisin, die an Geburtswehen stirbt. Ob im Tode mein Ich geboren wird? – ob ich im Jenseits werde, die ich bin?"

Und nach einer Pause hob sie noch einmal zu reden an. Jetzt schien ihre Stimme aus weiter Ferne zu kommen.

– "Ich höre das Schwanenlied, das die Sonne singt. Morgenröte!" Mit dem Ausdruck seligen Lauschens sank ihr Kopf leicht wie ein Hauch in die Kissen zurück. Ohne Alter, ohne Geschlecht war dieses sterbende Antlitz, in dem Tod und Schönheit sich vermählten. Die mächtig glanzvollen Augen, von dunklen Schatten umgeben, schienen durch Himmel und Erde hindurch ewige Zeiten und unendliche Räume zu durchmessen. Sie schienen zu sehen und zu verstehen, was im Diesseits nicht gesehen und verstanden wird. In ihrem Licht war ein Vergehen und Werden, ein Absterben und ein neues Leben, eine unermessliche Traurigkeit und ein begeistertes Schauen voll erhabenen Staunens.

Höher und höher stiegen die Augensterne, bis sie allmählich hinter den breiten Augenlidern verschwanden.

Ein Marmorbild von reiner Schönheit lag sie da im Tode, mit dem Blutstropfen auf der Stirn, auf dem Haupt die dornige Myrte.

The diary ended here. Doctor Behrend did not find in it what he had hoped to: psychological material on the development of mental illnesses. But he was deeply moved by human emotion as he approached the bedside of the dying woman. She sat upright. Her face was as thin as a shadow. She was still wearing the wilted myrtle wreath, its sharp stalks entangled in her hair. Someone had tried to remove it and scratched her in the process. A drop of blood trickled down her forehead. Mechanically, she picked apart the passionflower which lay on the blanket. Her eyes, captivated by Death, were fixed on the fireball of the setting sun. As she now addressed the doctor in a voice that resembled the echoing sounds of a harp, a gentle smile played around her lips: 'An old woman dying of the pains of childbirth. Will my Self be born in death? – will I become who I am in the hereafter?'

And after a pause, she began to speak again. Now her voice seemed to come from far away.

– 'I hear the swan song that the sun sings. The reddening dawn!' With an expression of blissful rapture, her head sank back into the pillows as lightly as a breath. Without age, without sex was this dying face, in which death and beauty were united. The powerful, shining eyes, surrounded by dark shadows, seemed to cut across the eternity of time and the infinity of space, through Heaven and Earth. They seemed to see and understand all that is not seen and understood in this world. In their light was a passing and a becoming, a death and a rebirth, an immeasurable sadness, and a raving gleam of sublime wonder.

The irises ascended higher and higher until they gradually disappeared behind large eyelids.

A marble statue of true beauty, she lay there in death, with the drop of blood on her brow and the myrtle wreath upon her head.

www.ingramcontent.com/pod-product-compliance
Lightning Source LLC
Chambersburg PA
CBHW070953120726
47910CB00004B/1218